Frederick William Robinson

Coward Conscience

Vol. III.

Frederick William Robinson

Coward Conscience
Vol. III.

ISBN/EAN: 9783337014094

Printed in Europe, USA, Canada, Australia, Japan

Cover: Foto ©Andreas Hilbeck / pixelio.de

More available books at **www.hansebooks.com**

COWARD CONSCIENCE.

BY

F. W. ROBINSON,

AUTHOR OF

"GRANDMOTHER'S MONEY," "LITTLE KATE KIRBY,"
&c., &c.

"O coward conscience, how dost thou afflict me!"
SHAKSPEARE.

IN THREE VOLUMES.
VOL. III.

LONDON:
HURST AND BLACKETT, PUBLISHERS,
13, GREAT MARLBOROUGH STREET.
1879.

LONDON:
PRINTED BY DUNCAN MACDONALD,
BLENHEIM HOUSE.

CONTENTS

OF

THE THIRD VOLUME.

BOOK III.—MISERERE.

(CONTINUED.)

CHAPTER		PAGE
V. Marcus receives Consolation	. .	3
VI. Lady Dagnell's Opinions	. . .	14
VII. The Two Together	. . . .	25
VIII. "God Speed"	. . . .	38
IX. One Good Action .	. . .	51
X. The Engaged Couple	. . . .	63
XI. Ghosts . .	. . . .	69
XII. Next Morning	. . . .	78
XIII. The Warning	. . . .	90
XIV. The Storm Bursts .	. . .	99
XV. Resolutions .	. . . .	110
XVI. More Questions	. . . .	120
XVII. Nearing the End .	. . .	128
XVIII. The other Room .	. . .	144
XIX. Requiescat in Pace	. . .	157

BOOK IV.—THE LINKS OF THE CHAIN.

CHAPTER		PAGE
I. Untimely Visitors	. . . .	173
II. Revelation	. . . .	188
III. After the Visit	. . . .	198
IV. The Old Servant	. . . .	209
V. The Last Meeting in their Lives	. .	217
VI. Mr. Harnett's Emporium	. .	232
VII. A New Resolution	. . .	246
VIII. Business	. . . . .	256
IX. Ursula's Instructions	. . .	263
X. Red silk Blinds	. . . .	276

BOOK III.

(CONTINUED.)

MISERERE.

COWARD CONSCIENCE.

CHAPTER V.

MARCUS RECEIVES CONSOLATION.

TOM DAGNELL turned the handle of the door and entered the apartment, which had been especially devoted to the use of his elder brother. Here Marcus, when suffering from headache, or disposed to escape from the frivolities of the drawing-room, or the complaints of his mother, would take refuge, and be seen no more by mortal eye. And here Marcus Dagnell was sitting with the window thrown up, and the cool summer air coming in across the park-land to him. There were two wax candles burning in the room and flickering in

the draught, which Marcus was facing with
bare throat, and in a manner totally opposed to
his usual precautionary method. There was an
open letter on the table, and Tom, after he had
closed the door behind him, guessed that the
bad news had reached his brother first.

"That is from Fanny," he said.

"Yes—take a seat, Tom," answered Marcus.
"I have some news for you."

"Spare yourself, old boy, I know everything."

"I don't really see how——"

"I have met Fanny and her husband on the
sands this evening."

"Oh! you have," said Marcus, after a slight
pause. "Are they quite well?"

"Quite well."

"That's all right;" and then Marcus was
silent, and content to stare at his brother, and
watch his preparations for finding a chair, and
drawing it towards him.

"I thought it was my task to break the
news to you," said Tom, "as this letter had
not reached Broadlands, I fancied."

"It came this morning," said Marcus, coolly.

"You have known it all day, then?"

"Yes, all day," answered Marcus.

"By Jove! I envy you your powers of self-command," exclaimed his brother. "Why, you are a stoic, Marcus! I was coming to console you—to say all this was for the best, and that it is lucky you have discovered Fanny does not care for you before marriage instead of afterwards."

"Tha-anks, Tom," responded Marcus, with his old drawl. "All that sort of thing is the usual kind of consolation, I suppose. It don't do any good, but one seems to expect it. Will you have a cigar?"

"Not to-night."

"I don't mind the smoke, and you are seldom without a cigar in your mouth at this time of night, are you?"

"I would rather not smoke," answered Tom.

"As you please."

Marcus relapsed into silence again, and fixed his gaze upon the opposite wall. Tom thought he was looking pale, and that there was an

extra degree of grimness on his countenance;
but, Marcus being always pale and grim, it
was difficult to note any material change in
him.

"Why did you not tell me this to-day?"
asked Tom.

"I thought I would leave it till the morning,"
was the reply. "There is no occasion for a
fuss."

"She is not worth making a fuss about,"
cried Tom, indignantly.

"She is a deuced fine girl," was his brother's
comment, "and would have suited me exactly.
I wonder what she saw in the other fellow,
Tom?"

"'Fifty thou.!' as her father calls it."

"Not she," replied Marcus; "she was not
thinking of money—that is not Fanny's style at
all."

"Perhaps it was the style of the man."

"Can't say, really," and Marcus looked
ahead of him, as if some hidden reason might
be inscribed amongst the scrolls of his flock
wall-paper.

"You are well quit of your bargain, Marcus. Such a woman would never have made you happy," said Tom. "It has always struck me how unsuited you were for each other."

Marcus's gaze wandered again from the wall-paper to his brother's sympathetic face.

"I don't see why that should strike you," said Marcus. "All matches are deuced odd, with the wrong ones coming together instead of the right. Sir John and our mother, for instance—you and Ursula—and everybody all round."

This was a long speech for Marcus, and out of his usual way. Tom felt disposed to wince, but he replied calmly—

"There are some odd couples in the world, certainly."

"By gad! there are," assented the elder brother. He picked up Fanny's letter and passed it over to his brother.

"Would you like to read it?"

"No; I should not," replied Tom.

"Why?"

"I can make a fair guess at its contents. I

know what such a spasmodic sentimentalist
would say," was Tom's answer.

"Very likely.   You are a clever fellow, Tom,
and used to this sort of thing.   I am a bit of
a muff," said Marcus, taking back his letter
and putting it in the breast-pocket of his
coat.

"Fanny wishes to see you to-morrow.   Is
that expressed in the missive?"

"Yes; oh, yes."

"I should not go, if I were you."

"I have not the slightest intention of going,"
Marcus drawled forth.   "She mentions half-
past nine in the morning, and a fellow cannot
get down to breakfast comfortably by that
time.   Besides——"

"Well?"

"Besides, I don't want to see her—much," he
concluded, gulping something down in his
throat.   "Upon my soul I don't, Tom, ever
any more!"

He clapped his thin white hands suddenly to
his eyes, as if fearful of some sign of human
weakness there of which he was ashamed,

and Tom laid his own strong hand upon his shoulder.

"Courage, Marcus; you are not the man to give way."

"It was a deuced shabby trick, Tom, wasn't it?" he murmured.

"Yes, but it is not worth grieving at."

"I'm not going to grieve," said Marcus, lowering his hands again; "I shall get over this about twenty minutes past ten. If I think of it any later I shan't have any sleep, and I'm an awful Guy Fawkes after a bad night's rest. I wish you would have a cigar," he said, pushing his case towards Tom again. "You don't seem the same man without one. It fidgets me, and I'm afraid of what you're going to say next."

Tom took a cigar, and lighted it at this second invitation.

"I'm not going to say anything more," said Tom. "I have congratulated you on your lucky escape, and there's an end of it."

"I answered her letter—she'll get it to-morrow morning," observed Marcus. "I said I thought it was an escape for us both—just your idea, you see."

"Bravo !"

"I did not send my compliments to Slither-wick," said Marcus. "I daresay he will feel a little hurt, but I couldn't do it !"

"In the old days you would have challenged him, and shot him through his sneaking carcase."

"Yes, or got shot myself," added Marcus, "but I don't think Fanny is worth dying for, just at present, or killing anybody else for. Besides, Slitherwick will make her a very good husband, and she will be very comfortable, and——"

"And you should be the happiest of the three of them," concluded Tom.

"I don't feel what you call jolly, just at present—it's come at me with such a left-hand-ed slap, Tom," said Marcus, "but still I am philosopher enough to know she wouldn't have been happy with me. She would have had that Slitherwick—beastly name, Slitherwick, isn't it ? —always on her mind, as the fellow she *did* care for."

" Yes, Marcus, that's it."

"Perhaps it will be a good lesson to you, Tom," said Marcus, slowly.

Tom took his cigar from his mouth, and stared almost with horror at his brother. Had this unlooked-for crisis in the career of Marcus Dagnell affected far more lives than his, and was the truth approaching at double-quick time, in consequence? He had been blind to the truth until to-night, perhaps wilfully blind; a child shutting its eyes to the facts which were there.

" What lesson do you mean ?" he inquired.

" I don't mean much," answered Marcus. " It has not been my business, and I never cared for other peoples'. But does not Ursula's position put you in mind of my own ?"

" Not at all," was the sharp reply. " Why should it ?"

" You don't care for her—you can't like her much. I don't know anybody who could, with her bad tempers. You——"

" It's all a fool's mistake," cried Tom, angrily. " Ursula is one of the best women in the world.

We should have been beggars long ago, had she not out of pure love for us all sunk every penny of her money to save an ungrateful lot from ruin."

"We're an ungrateful lot—yes," said Marcus, "and yet you are going to marry her out of gratitude—that's it."

"Why not out of love?"

"Because it seems to me you love the other girl," replied Marcus, thoughtfully; "and if you can tell Ursula so, just as Fanny has told me, so much the better, and the sooner the better, too. I don't think I would make a bolt of it, you know, as Slitherwick and Fanny did, for that's damned shabby; but I would tell Ursula."

"I have told Ursula I love her," answered Tom, "Do you think I am going to break her heart? Is that like me?"

"Don't worry me," pleaded the elder brother. "I don't mind what you do. I have only just mentioned my own idea, that's all. Very likely I am wrong. I often am, and, if you are going to make a fuss over this, don't make it here, there's a good fellow. My head will not stand that kind of thing to-night."

" I beg pardon, Marcus," said Tom, " I'm in a noisy mood, and you have astonished me a little. But why you should think that, having pledged my solemn faith to one, I could——Marcus," he exclaimed, " I shall marry Ursula, and very shortly. You will see that for yourself. I don't break my word like these Olivers."

" All right. Shut the door, Tom, if you are going, and thank you for dropping in to cheer me up a bit."

" Don't mention it," said Tom, somewhat gruffly.

" It is the right sort of thing to marry the one you care most for," added Marcus ; " that's my consolation—that's yours. Don't forget to shut the door behind you. Good night."

Tom went away, and, when the door was closed, Marcus took from his pocket Fanny's letter, and read it very attentively once more. That was his own business at least, and it was not easy to shake it from his mind.

CHAPTER VI.

LADY DAGNELL'S OPINIONS.

TOM went downstairs to the drawing-room, after a moment's hesitation in the corridor, as if half disposed to see his father, or seek the repose and peace of his own apartment. He had a great deal to reflect upon, but he did not care for more reflection ; he preferred action to thought, the impulse of the moment to the cool deliberation of the night. There had been a great deal to disturb him that evening, and he was scarcely his usual self. To think that Marcus's little love-affair should have unsettled him completely, given him new thoughts, and put such extraordinary ideas, too, into poor Marcus's confused brain!

In the drawing-room he found his mother and
Violet Hilderbrandt. Ursula had withdrawn to
break the news to Sir John, and to console him,
if there should arise any necessity for consolation, and Lady Dagnell had received all the
information from our heroine. The ill-news
had flown apace throughout the establishment;
the domestics, by that rapid method for the
dissemination of details which is known only
to themselves, were already discussing the
position in the servants' hall; it would be
known half over Sussex before to-morrow's
sundown.

Lady Dagnell was excited by the incident
which had removed her for a while from her
own peculiar sphere of self, and given her fresh
thoughts.

"To think, Thomas, that Fanny should have
acted in so unladylike a fashion!" she exclaimed, as her son entered—"quite indelicate, wholly
unnecessary, and altogether inexcusable."

"Violet has told you?" said Tom.

It was no longer Miss Hilderbrandt with any
of the Dagnells; the family had claimed her,

and all formality of address had been discarded in these latter days.

"You will not scold me for being so ready with bad tidings," said Violet to him. "It was Ursula's wish that I shonld tell Lady Dagnell."

"Marcus will be obliged by your saving him the trouble," replied Tom. "As for the tidings, why do you call them bad? I have been congratulating my brother on his good luck."

"I don't often agree with you," said the mother, "but I think you are right for once. He is well rid of this Oliver connection, and Fanny was not worthy of becoming a Dagnell, and a daughter of mine. In a monetary point of view it was what vulgar people might term 'a good catch,' but I am not distressed at the result. There was no blood in the Olivers, and no good breeding, which is next to blood— sometimes before it, although I prefer blood myself."

"Is this Lady Dagnell, or Lady Macbeth talking so murderously?" inquired Tom, with a laugh, in which neither of his listeners joined.

The effort to add a lightness to the proceedings was a terrible failure at that time. It was no laughing matter to the mother for a Dagnell to be treated so unfairly as Marcus had been, and, though a woman of many faults and failings, still she was a mother in her little way.

"Don't be frivolous, Thomas, there is nothing to laugh at that I can perceive," was Lady Dagnell's icy remark, "and I am sure Violet is not in the mood for jesting either. She has felt this very much, very acutely, I may say, and has been dreadfully dull all the evening. She has not amused me in the least; she has not touched the piano; she has talked of nothing but Marcus."

Tom looked towards Violet. Yes, she was very pale, and there was a sadness in her face that reminded him of the Birmingham days, when friends were scarce and life was full of pit-falls. Why should she be distressed at this so much? In what way did it affect her? For what reason was she—no matter how gentle, amiable and sensitive—to take this to heart almost as if it were a trouble of her own? Surely impos-

sible!—and yet he was almost certain there
had been tears shed over it, or over something
to which this had given rise. It was the old
face of doubt and distress which had awakened
his sympathy before the mystery of her life had
been revealed to him. Revealed!—after all,
what did he know of it? and of her thoughts,
how many?

Violet became aware of Tom Dagnell's close
survey of her, and the red colour flickered
to her cheeks.

"I—I thought this might be a trouble," she
stammered forth, " to Marcus, to Lady Dagnell,
even to you, his brother. But I am not sure
now. It is as well they should not have been
married, perhaps."

"Perhaps!" exclaimed Tom, with more force
of expression than he had intended, or was
aware of—with more surprise even, though
there was little to astonish him in what Violet
had said, which sounded like a far-away echo of
his own words to Marcus.

"I have been thinking of Ursula's opinion,"
explained Violet, "and," she added, "I have

been disturbed by it. Miss Oliver should have kept her word at any cost, Ursula thought. It was a contract solemnly entered into between her and your brother—it had been ratified by her family and yours—it was very dishonourable for her, as it would have been for him, to turn away at the eleventh hour. I see all this with Ursula very plainly."

"That is Ursula's view of it, then?" asked Tom.

"Yes."

"And yet it may be for the best that they have parted, *you* think?" continued Tom.

There was a strange appealing glance towards him, but he did not heed it, or in all respects comprehend it. He was only anxious to know what Violet Hilderbrandt thought in her own heart of all that they had heard that day, and when she remained silent, he repeated, almost mercilessly, his question.

"Yes, I think so," Violet replied at last. "There could have been no happiness to them —everything would have been so false, and misery would have followed very quickly."

"Yes, partly," said Tom, "but they had decided to share their lives together—they were not boy and girl—and one of them, at least, might have been always happy in ignorance of the truth."

"I do not believe in happy ignorance," affirmed Lady Dagnell. "There would have been a discovery—possibly a more discreditable elopement than this—and all kinds of dreadful scandal afterwards. I am very glad Miss Oliver has settled it in this fashion, so far as I am concerned. though why she couldn't have told Marcus when he was at Birmingham, or have got rid of this Mr. Slitherwick when he first became attentive, I cannot comprehend. But to go on with the two of them—till the very last —it's absolutely disgraceful, when one comes to think of it."

"Yes," said Tom, moodily, "there's not much excuse for Fanny Oliver, poor girl."

"Poor girl, indeed!" cried his mother. "I don't see anything to pity in her, Thomas. I wonder what Sir John thinks of it. If I thought he would not upset me with bad language, I would go upstairs and talk to him."

"Ay, do, mother," said Tom, "and Ursula can join us for a while."

"Ursula has been out all the evening with you," said Lady Dagnell, "and cannot neglect her uncle any more. She must not allow selfish thoughts to interfere with her duty. Besides, I'm not going to be shut up alone with Sir John in one of his terrible tempers."

"There's Mrs. Coombes."

"Sir John is not afraid of Mrs. Coombes," replied Lady Dagnell. "When you and Ursula were at Birmingham he flung his broth-basin at her; she has no power to restrain his violence. Ursula has."

"But he is not violent to-night," said Tom. "He may be sorry—he thought this so good a match for Marcus—he——"

"My dear son, don't run on like that; it distresses me," implored Lady Dagnell. "I have not made up my mind to visit Sir John. Why don't you go yourself, if you are anxious about your father this evening?"

"I don't wish to talk of this to him," was

Tom's measured reply. "I am tired of the subject."

"Where's Marcus?" asked his mother.

"I would not disturb him," Tom replied; "he has gone to his own room, out of our way."

"I think I'll see Sir John for a few minutes," Lady Dagnell said. "Ring for my maid to assist me up the stairs. If I don't return again, good night to you both."

"Pray lean upon my arm," said Violet. "Let me accompany——"

"No, thank you, my dear," replied Lady Dagnell, quite graciously. "You will stay and keep my son company. He must not be quite alone in this house to-night, he is not himself, I see. All this has upset you very much, Thomas. I don't know why. I can't attempt to guess why, but it has. Try to be more cheerful to-morrow, please. The establishment is dismal enough without your adding to the gloom which weighs me down so shockingly. Good night."

The maid entered the room, and Lady Dagnell took her arm and departed on her strange quest, as Tom innocently imagined. But Lady Dagnell was as eccentric as the rest of the family, as changeable in her moods, and as seriously unsettled. She went straight to her room without a second thought of her lord and master, or of the effect upon his mind which Fanny's secret marriage might have had. A suspicious person would have fancied that Lady Dagnell had invented an excuse to leave these young folk together, was anxious even that they should be together for reasons best known to herself.

Had he followed her ladyship to her own boudoir, he would have been confirmed in his suspicions—he would have been startled even at the degree of intimacy existing between Lady Dagnell and her maid.

"Here's your cordial, my lady," was the maid's remark, "it's a leetle stronger than usual, but you're rather sad to-night."

Lady Dagnell took her cordial almost greedily, and disposed of it forthwith. There was a strong aroma of brandy in the room during the process.

" You haven't seen Miss Dagnell anywhere ?" asked the mistress.

"No, my lady. She's boxed up with Sir John, and quite safe."

" That's well," said Lady Dagnell, spitefully. " Little does she think I have left the two of them together. Potter, I would rather anyone should have my son than Miss Ursula—you know I hate her, Potter, don't you ?"

" Yes, my lady, I have heard you say so before."

" She rules the house as if it were her own; she weakens my authority, and pays no respect to it; she frightens me as to what she will be as my son's wife," muttered Lady Dagnell. " She—Potter, do you think a little more support would do me any harm to-night, I am very weak and low ?"

" Lor' bless your ladyship, no !"

" Half a glass more, then. This has been a trying day for me."

CHAPTER VII.

THE TWO TOGETHER.

FRIENDS as they were, brother and sister as to all appearances Tom Dagnell and Violet had become, it was a moment of embarrassment to both of them when Lady Dagnell and her maid had withdrawn, and they were together in the drawing-room. What was at the heart of each, each knew, and why it throbbed thus painfully with the sense of being alone together —with the fear of what words might escape to alter every thought of theirs from that night forth.

A memorable night—a crisis unduly precipitated by Fanny Oliver's romance, which was the lighting of the train, despite all efforts to go on blindfolded to the end, along the path of insecurity.

If Lady Dagnell bore malice in her heart for the past contempt, past slights of Ursula, she had well calculated the hour of her revenge upon her.

Violet had remained standing after Lady Dagnell had withdrawn; she was anxious to escape; there was a new timidity upon her which was very striking.

"Will you not sit down again?" Tom asked.

"I—I think I will bid you good night," was the answer. "It is getting late."

"My mother's wishes were that you should keep me company, Violet," he said, in a low voice.

"But——"

"And I want to speak to you for a little while longer. Don't go yet."

"To speak to me?" she repeated, nervously. "Is there any——"

"About Marcus, that's all," he added, quickly; "for this brother, and this brother's position, trouble me."

Violet sat down thus adjured—and thus re-
assured. But it was a dangerous topic, and led
on to danger.

"The whole thing haunts me, Violet," said
Tom, restlessly; "it is on my conscience as if I
were not acting well, and knew not how to act
—as if I were a coward!"

Violet half rose in her chair, alarmed by this
sudden outburst, but at his imploring gestures
she resumed her seat.

"Only to speak of Marcus, understand, and
how he troubles me!" he entreated. "You
think it is best that he and Fanny are apart?"

"It must surely be for the best."

"But what is your opinion?"

"I don't know," confessed Violet; "it should
be for the best that those who—who do not
love each other, should go their separate ways,
but I—I don't know. There are so many reasons for so many lives, and I have not thought
of this."

"Ursula thinks to the contrary," said Tom.
'Once a promise, even to the risk of one's soul,
should be always a promise to be faithfully

performed. She has said as much as that to you ?"

" She has."

" Well, is she right or not ?"

" I would not answer hastily to such a question. I should want time to think it out for myself," was the guarded answer.

" With Marcus and Fanny—one cold and phlegmatic, and the other frivolous and shallow —it matters not much either way," said Tom, "and disturbs not the argument. But if Marcus had been a man of one idea, and that idea his love for Fanny Oliver—if he had built the whole happiness of his life upon her promise, and felt he might die if she were to break her word with him, what then ? Would it not be more honourable and merciful to keep her word—would she not be happy in time, knowing her conduct had been strictly honourable towards him ?"

"It is possible," murmured Violet; "it is probable."

" You would commend her as a heroine ?" he asked.

"Yes, I would," was the quick answer.

"Because she would give up her own happiness—her love for some one else, you see, to save one poor heart from breaking. And that is heroic. We read a great deal of this sort of thing—in books!" Tom added, bitterly, "and we should take our example from such goodly teaching. But in real life—it's a hard task."

"Marcus will not take this seriously to heart, you have said," answered Violet, "and so what does it matter? I—I will go to my room," she added, rising again, pale and afraid of him; and this time he made no effort to arrest her progress. He rose with her and said,

"I am not thinking of Marcus. I was——"

"No, no; don't tell me."

"I am thinking of Ursula—of myself; and how foolish I have been!"

"No, no; I will not hear it," cried Violet, hastening towards the door. "You are treacherous to Ursula. Don't tell me any more; try to love her as you promised. She is already most unhappy!"

"Has she said so?" he asked. "Has she owned it?"

"Yes."

"To-night?"

"Yes, to-night."

"Before you reached home this evening?" was his next eager question.

"Yes," answered Violet for the third time.

"She should have told me this, not you," cried Tom, following her to the door and reaching it before her. "She has not been fair with you."

"No matter, Tom," she answered, "I am going away to-morrow. God forbid I should stay here any longer!"

"Going away! Where?"

"I do not know. But I am going away," she answered, helplessly.

"At her command,—at her orders?"

"At my own wish," was the reply. "I am only anxious to go, to prove——"

She stopped, and Tom said, in a deep voice,

"Well?"

"No; what is the use of it? Let me pass, please; don't stand in my way like an enemy!" she cried, more angrily.

Tom stepped aside, but as she made a movement to pass him he held her lightly by the wrist.

· "Does Ursula distrust you, Violet?" he asked, in a hoarse voice, "is she jealous?"

"I—I fear she is."

"You must go away, then," said Tom, sorrowfully. "And if I had never seen you, mine would have been a happier and a better life!"

"Oh! don't say that," cried Violet.

"Ursula is quite right to part us, for—I love you, Violet! I can't help it now—I have been fool enough to deceive myself, and like a fool I am punished. But I love you," he replied, "and you may as well know the whole truth, and despise me for once and all."

"Why should I despise you?"

"I have broken my word. I have asked the woman I can't love to marry me, and I have turned to you as the only woman who can save me."

"Don't say any more, for Heaven's sake, Tom, not another word," and Violet put her hands to her ears, as if to shut all sound from them. "Think of poor Ursula!"

"You are going away, and I shall be alone here! So I speak out, lest there be an error or mistake between us. If you had only loved me, I would have gone to Ursula, and begged her to consider what was best. I would have knelt to her to set me free—I would have implored her to remember how she was noble and unselfish for my old father's sake, and how it would be a greater mercy to give me back my promise."

"She loves you—loves you madly, and like a madwoman," cried Violet. "You must think of her—not me. Good-bye."

"Why, you are crying!"

"Let me pass. Oh, how cruel you are!"

"Go now," said Tom; "God bless you, Violet. In the morning I will see you again; I shall be stronger then," he added, seeing the look of fear upon her face; "I shall be my old self. You will not have any occasion to be afraid of me."

"I was never afraid of you," said Violet,

smiling faintly through her tears, "until to-night. And I am very, very sorry that I have stood between you and your cousin. I did not mean it. It is a poor return for her kindness and yours."

" No."

" She says so ; and she is wiser than we are," said Violet. "She has read your heart more quickly than its owner. But have I—oh! have I in any way sought to win your affection from her, Tom ?"

" No."

" She says I have."

" By Heaven ! she is wrong," he exclaimed. "It is my own fault—my own selfishness."

" Tell her so, when I am gone, and she will think the better of me."

" I will. But," he added, with a new dis-trust, "you will not leave this house without my knowledge. There must be no more mystery."

" No, I will not steal away like a thief," she answered. " Good night."

" Good night," he echoed. Then she put her

hand in his, and he raised it suddenly to his
lips and kissed it passionately many times,
until she struggled away and vanished like a
vision from him.

He paced up and down the room, long after
she had gone, more like a wild beast than a
man, and with the heavy iron bars before his
cage, and Violet in the free air and sunshine.
and for ever set beyond him. And he had
acted like a wild beast, cruelly and ungrate-
fully—and to both women, sparing neither in
his unmanly passion and mad impulses. He
would tell Ursula all—there was the one solution to the great enigma—with or without
Violet he would not shrink from the truth. He
had told Fanny only that night upon the sands
that he would not be afraid to meet it, and here
it was before him like a wall, within an hour or
two of his assertion.

Yes, he would tell Ursula everything. Now,
this very instant, and end the farce of it, or
the grim tragedy of it, upon which the black
curtain was descending, He should find Ursula

in his father's room—ever on the watch, poor
Ursula, and ever to be rewarded by ingrati-
tude.

He could not help that now, for Ursula suspected him! She *was* terribly wise, she had read
his heart like an open page, it would be no surprise to her, and only a bitter humiliation for
himself.

She would forgive him, for he was penitent,
and she loved him very much. And true love
is always generous, if desperately jealous.

He did not hesitate. With the same haste as
he had descended the stairs one March night to
ask her to be his wife, he went swiftly up them
to make his recantation, to own his passion for
another woman! He had always acted in hot
haste, but surely this was the right course—the
only honourable course—to pursue? The
whole truth! And Ursula herself to decide
what was best!

In the corridor, he met Mrs. Coombes.

" Miss Dagnell is with my father, I suppose?"
he said.

"She has gone to her room, sir."

"Are you sure?"

"Almost. Sir John said she was coming back directly, to sit with him, and that I might go to my room."

"Is Sir John asleep?"

"Drowsy like, sir. That's all."

"I will stay with him till Miss Dagnell returns. Good night."

"Good night, sir."

Tom went softly into the room, lest his father should be asleep, and closed the door after him. All was very still and silent, as if the father were dead almost. He passed round the screen, where was nothing but an empty chair planted before a steel grate, which was full of blackened and charred coals, a fire dead of neglect.

"Not here," said Tom—then he stole towards the adjoining bed-room and peered round the door. The heavy damask hangings hid the bed from view, and he approached, still wondering—and growing cold with fear as he proceeded. It was all so quiet! He drew the curtains aside, but the bed was untenanted, and smooth and white as the nurse had left it in the morning.

Sir John Dagnell was not there.

CHAPTER VIII.

" GOD SPEED."

TOM DAGNELL was hardly certain he was
in complete possession of his faculties—that
he might not be even dreaming at the moment,
and the victim of extraordinary delusions.
There had come so rapid an onrush of events
towards him since the day's beginning, that it
was easy to believe it was all part of a fevered
sleep from which he should wake presently.

The walk upon the Littlehampton sands with
the sky all gold and crimson above him, and
people whom he had seen last at Birmingham
confronting him and telling him strange truths
which appertained to their lives and yet influ-
enced his own—the figure of Marcus afterwards,

desolate and grief-stricken, or a something like Marcus, but not so cold and angular—the white face of Ursula watching him up the stairs, and Violet shrinking from his love as from a blow, and praying for his silence—and now the empty rooms which had been the sick father's province for many weary months and where there was no sick father to receive him, seemed all torn fragments of a dream, telling of nothing save that his imagination was disordered, and it would be a mercy to be back again in his old matter of-fact world.

Still he was scarcely walking in his sleep, and this was surely his father's apartment. His pulse was at fever-beat, born of the heart-storms which had raged within him, and had swept away the miserable conventionalities about him. He *had* struggled from his prison, and cast himself free from his chains; he *had* told Violet Hilderbrandt he loved her, and he was in search of Ursula, whom he had never loved,—to whom he would make confession now, and ask for absolution, on his bended knees, if she required it. A man in search of truth, that he had to find out for himself, just as the gun-maker's wife had prophesied, little thinking how close the truth was to him, and what a lowering spectre it would prove.

Yes, he was awake. It had all happened; this was no illusion, only a new wave of mystery breaking upon the shore, whereon he stood facing the storm, and feeling he was not so strong to cope with it as in the days gone by.

The absence of his father bewildered him for awhile, but it took his thoughts somewhat from Violet and Ursula, and led him to strive vainly to account for Sir John Dagnell's disappearance. He walked into the front room again to make sure his senses had not failed him, and that his father was really absent—he even drew aside the thick curtains before the entrance door, and looked behind them, like a child suspecting a playmate of a trick to scare him.

" Not here," muttered Tom. " I will call Mrs. Coombes."

He went into the corridor, glanced right and

left of him, and became aware of a shuffling figure in the distance moving towards him in great haste, and with both hands extended, as if enjoining him to silence.

It was Fisher, the butler, advancing as rapidly as his feeble old legs would permit.

"Where is my father?" asked our hero. "Do you know he has left his room—what is the meaning of it all?"

"Hush! hush! for the Lord's sake don't make a noise, Master Tom!"

"My father——"

"He is quite right—he would go. After Miss Ursula had left he called me in to help to wrap him up, and take care of him, just as I used to do," said Fisher.

"You old fool, where is he?" exclaimed Tom, passionately.

"He is talking to Miss Hilderbrandt."

"To whom?"

"To Miss Hilderbrandt—he would see her."

"And Miss Ursula—Mrs. Coombes?"

"They know nothing of it, bless your soul," said the old man, with a chuckle.

" What does he want with Miss Hilderbrandt at this hour?"

"Ah! that's more than I can tell." said Fisher, " but he was very curious like to see her."

" Why didn't you come to me before he took this step?"

" He would not let me—and he would have gone without any help at all, if I hadn't been handy."

" I will follow him."

" No, don't do that, please," urged the old man; " he's very comfortable, sitting in her room; he's well wrapped up about the throat, and talking cool and quiet. It's a little whim of his—let him have it, sir. He won't have many more of 'em in this world."

Tom paused at this appeal.

" What can he possibly have to say?" he said again. " Why does he risk his life by seeing her?"

" He risks nothing, Master Tom, if you don't excite him by fetching him back," the butler re-marked. " He's as quiet as a lamb; it's a little change, and doing him a sight of good."

"How do you know?" asked our hero, sharply.

"When he leaned on my arm in the corridor, he walked quite strong and firm—as he used to do before he was took."

"You were in the way, you say?"

"Yes, handy like," Robin replied.

"It strikes me, Fisher, you are for ever on the prowl," said Tom, suspiciously.

"I'm pleased to see everything is safe about the house," Mr. Fisher said, apologetically, "and I don't rest very much myself."

"Neither can I rest, old man," said Tom, pushing him lightly aside, "I must see all is fair play here."

"Why, you don't——"

"I never trusted Sir John Dagnell," said Tom, sternly; then he walked sharply along the corridor, followed at a little distance by the butler, still appealing to him in a low, excited tone, for his father's sake, his own.

As Tom approached Violet Hilderbrandt's room the door opened, and saved him from following his own course. He stopped, and to his new amazement Violet came forth, with the old man leaning on her arm for support. They were two grave figures of youth and age, health and sickness, advancing towards him slowly, regarding him calmly even, as if his presence there was no matter of surprise to them.

"Your father has been good enough to pay me a visit," Violet said in explanation. "He has heard I am going away to-morrow."

"Who has told him?"

"Ursula."

"A guest in my house so long," said the father, "and I not able to see her—to wish her God speed on her journey. It was so very hard upon me, Tom, that I could not bear it any longer."

Tom glanced from his father to Violet, and he fancied that both looked away, as if both were hiding a new mystery from him.

"Take my arm, father," said Tom, "we will not trouble Miss Hilderbrandt further to-night."

"Thank you," he said to his son, "perhaps

you will be more support to me than this young
lady. Not that I want support to-night—I'm
getting strong again so fast."

"There, Master Tom, what did I say?" exclaimed the butler, as Sir John Dagnell took his
son's arm. "Doesn't he walk strong and firm
now?"

"No," was Tom's flat contradiction.

"Then he's given way again somewhere,"
said Fisher, stooping and looking at Sir John's
extremities critically. "Not that I ever thought
it would last. This is a mere flash like, o'
course."

"You're a croaking idiot," remarked Sir
John; "and I shall last longer than you by a
good six months, at least. Send him away,
Tom—strike him with this stick."

But Mr. Fisher did not wait to be struck, had
Tom even had an idea of assaulting the old
servant, who elevated his hands, and his shaggy
white eyebrows, and then shuffled away towards the staircase. Tom and his father proceeded towards the deserted sick-room, Violet
still walking slowly by the old man's side, the

butler in the distance standing now and watching them.

At the door Sir John turned to her again.

"I said 'God speed you on your journey,' I think?" he asked.

"Yes, Sir John," was the reply, "you did."

"God speed you once more—and *good speed*," he murmured.

They passed into the room, and Violet entered with them. Was this reality, or dreamland, after all? It was so like dreamland, and to be reconciled only by its laws—whatever they were—that Tom thought it might fade at any moment, and fresh faces, of the living and the dead together, perhaps, might be looking on them presently.

He led his father to the chair, wherein the old knight sank, and breathed hard—a man tired out with a long journey. His face was changed too—there was a new look upon it which was not always there, and the mouth was somewhat drawn. Violet leaned forwards and looked anxiously at him, as if there were a fear upon her for his life.

"He was unwise to visit me," she said to
Tom; "I did not think of seeing him."

"I was obliged to come," murmured the old
man. "There was no one else whom I could
trust."

"Your son?" suggested Violet.

"He was not to be found, and I could not
have trusted him either. He," said Sir John,
with his brow contracting as he spoke, "would
have asked a hundred questions, and worried
me to death. He is always asking questions!"

"Don't ask him any now, Tom," whispered
Violet. "Let him rest till the morning, will
you?"

"Yes," answered Tom.

"In the morning you will understand why he
called upon me," said Violet. "At least, I think
it will not be difficult to guess. Good-bye, Sir
John; you have been a good friend to me, and
I thank you, sir, with all my heart."

She stooped and kissed him on his wrinkled
forehead; then walked slowly and with head
bowed down towards the door, where she
stopped again and looked back—this time at

the man who had told her that he loved her.

"You will not leave your father?" she said.

"Not till Ursula comes."

"Not till Ursula comes," she repeated, then she wrung her hands together and turned from him.

Tom was once more at her side.

"You are going away," he said; "you will steal from me, after all."

"Your father wishes it."

"He has been set on by Ursula; they are plotting against you; they are driving you from the house."

"Ursula knows nothing of this."

"You promised me you would remain."

"Ah! an hour ago!" she answered, "but there, I have nowhere to go—and no friends beyond this place."

"I have been thinking—planning. I——"

She held up her hand, and he was silent at her gesture.

"I shall not mar your life ever again," she said. "You will not think or plan for me any more."

"I will live for no one else but you," he cried.

Again she shrank away from him, as she had done downstairs at an earlier hour of the night, and the face became more pallid on the instant.

"I frighten you," he said, with a low groan.

"Don't look grieved, Tom," she said. "I am not angry with you, nor afraid. I—I have never felt offended at your love for me. I shall never forget how good you have always been."

Yes, all this was surely a wild dream, and only to be reconciled by the inconsistencies that live in dreams. He was sure of it now!— it was impossible that this was Violet Hilderbrandt who came close to him, put two hands upon his shoulders, and looked at him sadly from her dark eyes' depths. This *was* a dream-figure!

"You will understand to-morrow why I kiss you, Tom. For the first and last time in my life!" she murmured.

Her lips touched his lightly as she spoke, and then, with her white face crimsoned, she fled from him along the corridor.

"Violet!" he cried, and at the same moment his father said, in a weaker, fainter voice—

"Tom, don't leave me!"

The curtain dropped before the door and hid away Tom's lady-love, and the son returned quickly to his father's side.

CHAPTER IX.

ONE GOOD ACTION.

YES, there was a change in Sir John Dagnell. He had not acted judiciously in proceeding in search of Violet Hilderbrandt; the fatigue had been too much for him. The breath was short and quick still, and the eyes looked strangely at the charred coals, as if wondering why the fire had gone out in his absence.

"You are ill," said Tom, anxiously.

"No worse than usual; a little tired, that is all."

"Shall I tell Mrs. Coombes——"

"No, no; damn Mrs. Coombes! You stay with me. I only want you."

"Ursula will not be very long, I suppose?"

"I don't want her to-night. I don't think she will come. When you see her, you must not say," he added, "I have been out of my room. She must not know that."

"Why?"

"When I'm worse, some day, I'll tell you why," he said. "You promised the girl you would not ask me any questions."

"True."

There was a silence of several minutes after this, during which the old man sat studying his fire-grate, and Tom, with folded arms and knit brows, endeavoured to work out the problem for himself, his heart meanwhile beating very fast. This was not the time to be sitting idly there, he thought; the time for action of some kind had come, and it was folly to remain supine. And yet how powerless he was to act! He knew not what to do, or what was threatening him and others. Violet was not going away, and still she had kissed him of her own free will and in all sad affection, as though she were parting from him for ever, and would leave a fair remembrance behind her. He would know all to-morrow, Violet had said; he would know all some day, his father had prophesied. Which was right in this strange reckoning?

"It is time you went to your room," said Tom, suddenly breaking away from his own thoughts; "it is too late to be sitting up."

Sir John did not fall in with this suggestion, but answered, in a slow, mechanical fashion:

"I intend to sit up to-night."

"But——"

"Ursula lets me remain here all night sometimes," he went on, "and when it would tire me too much to move."

"You are very tired, then?" asked Tom.

"Very."

"Why did you not send for Miss Hilderbrandt, if it were necessary you should see her?" asked Tom.

"There you go again,—more questions!" muttered the father.

"I forgot. Forgive me," said Tom, hastily.

Sir John's head was raised from its sunken position on his chest, at this.

"To think I should have anything to forgive," he said. "That is remarkable. Well,—I forgive you."

He held his wasted hands, as if for warmth, towards the grate again, and Tom said—

"You are cold. Some one must light this fire, if you really intend to remain."

"No, no," said Sir John, hastily. "I don't want anybody to come in again, to-night. I won't have anyone. *I'm* not cold—not very cold, that is."

"Mrs. Coombes said Ursula was coming back almost immediately."

"I did not know that."

"She said you told her so," Tom added.

"I wanted to get rid of her—to get away to Hilderbrandt's daughter—an old friend's daughter. I always liked Paul," he muttered. "A fellow of no principle, but with one of the best hearts in the world. Odd, wasn't it?"

"Very odd," was Tom's reply.

"And so awfully clever, that he frightened me at last," said Sir John, "for he——there you go again," he added, fretfully. "Trying to worm everything out of me. Why can't you let me rest ?"

"I am silent, father."

"Put something round my shoulders, and give me some brandy and water, and don't sit there like a stone statue. If you had been half a son," he said, "you would have tried to light the fire for me. You would have been doing it for yourself at Honfleur, if I had not been badgered into sending for you home."

This was an unkind cut from Sir John, but his son was not affected by it. Tom listened and carried out his father's instructions, but his thoughts were of the girl who had quitted him, and to whom his strong love had leaped forth that night in spite of all restraint. He wrapped a shawl round his father's shoulders; he mixed some weak brandy and water for him; he managed with a little difficulty to relight the fire, and, when all his labours were accomplished, Sir John Dagnell fancied he was well enough to go to bed now.

It was the mere expression of an idea, however; he dozed off to sleep the instant afterwards, and his son thought it was not safe to wake him. The knight was tired with his journey, and rest anywhere would do him good. What a time Ursula was absent, and why did she keep away, and where was she? And when she came back, would it be wise, and at that late hour, to tell her the whole truth which he had been burning to reveal only a little while ago? Would not truth keep till the early morning?

Poor cousin! She already guessed much of it? She had told Violet Hilderbrandt to quit Broadlands, for she was jealous of her. There was not much to reveal; it was only the shock of a confession from his own lips of his unworthiness that was to strike her down. How was it he had acted so badly, and in so weak a fashion? He had always plumed himself on the uprightness of his character, his keen sense of honour, his strict truthfulness,—and he had deceived Ursula Dagnell completely by his semblance of affection. The woman who had done so much for him—for them all—was alone to suffer, was to be treated worse than anyone else—to be set aside, if possible, from any further thought of his! Heaven help him; what an ingrate he was! Ursula was in her room sobbing out her life and love together. That was the story. She knew all now, and could not face him yet. Presently he should see her, with the bright glasses before her dry grey eyes, and her heart for ever shut against him as it deserved to be, and as he, God forgive him, wished it! It was his just punishment to be hated by Ursula—for no one but himself could guess what an immeasurable love he had for Violet Hilderbrandt, and how it had all flamed out at last, with the lava and hot ashes round about his path, and the dead hopes of others burnt up by the way.

Suddenly his father woke again, and with senses more acute than those of his thoughtful son.

"Tom, there is some one in the corridor," he said; "some one who is crying."

"Ursula!" exclaimed Tom. He went hastily to the door and opened it to discover Cabbage on the mat outside, sniffling and whining, and evidently in great perturbation of spirit.

"It's Cab," he said to his father; "he has crept upstairs to-night."

"He never comes here," muttered Sir John. "Don't let the beast into the room : he might fly at my throat in a minute."

"Poor old Cab, you must go back !" said Tom. "You are as wakeful as the rest of us to-night, it seems."

Cab, conscious that he was entrenching on forbidden ground, and yet anxious to attract the notice of his young master, writhed upon his stomach towards Tom, licked the hand that patted him, and whined piteously, and like a child.

Tom started back and said,

"The dog is wet; he has been in the sea."

"I wish he had been drowned there !" growled Sir John.

Tom shut out Cabbage in the corridor after an injunction to go downstairs, which Cab immediately obeyed, leaving a long trail of water behind him. Tom stood with his hand upon the curtains reflecting upon this, and half

disposed to follow Cabbage, a remembrance of
the night of the robbery at Mr. Oliver's coming
to him sharply, though it was difficult to asso-
ciate the dog's wet condition with any idea of
burglary, until our hero had returned to
the fireside and discovered blood upon his
hand.

" Something has happened to Cab! The dog
is hurt!" he exclaimed. " One moment, Sir
John."

He had left the room, and was downstairs in
the hall before Sir John could urge a protest
against his departure. In a few minutes he
had returned. Sir John was wide awake and
inquisitive.

" Well." he said, earnestly, " what have you
discovered?"

" Old Fisher asleep on the hall stairs."

" Drunk, I daresay." was Sir John's comment.

" No, he is sober enough. I woke him and
told him to be off to bed. He had heard no
noise, he said; the house is securely fastened,
and nothing has happened since I have been
here."

" What did you think had happened ?"

" The dog is wet—has been in the sea or the Arun, and has got hurt. How did Cab enter the house again ?" said Tom.

" There, that's just like you," remarked the querulous father—" more questions, as if I knew anything of the dog, as if I could tell, as if I cared."

" I did not expect you to tell me," said Tom. " Try to rest, father, it is late."

" Is that rain against the window ?" inquired Sir John.

" Yes, it is raining fast," replied Tom ; " there is a storm without."

" A miserable night !" remarked Sir John. " And the sea bellows most infernally. I don't think I shall sleep to-night, tired as I am."

He drew the shawl closely round his neck and shoulders with his wasted hands ; it was a dull, red India shawl, and the face looked very ghastly by contrast with its colour. Tom was not sure his father was so well, but the voice was sharper and clearer than its wont, and the mind worked on still and kept him wakeful.

"Strange he does not ask for Ursula," thought Tom—"that he does not seem to miss her."

"Tom," he said, suddenly again, and when our hero had hoped he was dozing, "are you there?"

"Yes," was the reply.

"If I should not think of it again—if I should not have a chance of alluding to it, I want you to remember something," said Sir John.

"Go on; I am listening."

"I have done one good action in my life—a good, sound, unselfish action."

"Many of them, I hope, father. Yours has been a long life."

"Yes; but I haven't done any good in it. I see that pretty plainly to-night, if I never did before. How do you account for that?" he inquired.

"I cannot account for it."

"I did one good action in visiting Miss— Miss——"

He hesitated for the name, and Tom supplied it.

" Hilderbrandt," he said.

" Yes, Hilderbrandt. Why did I forget that
name, now? My memory is going, Tom, by
God! To forget that man's name is a bad
sign for me," he said. " I'm not so well, I'm
sure I'm not so well."

" Pure fancy, sir."

" But I'll not excite myself to-night about it.
Don't make any further uproar, Tom, will you?
I'll try to sleep."

Sir John Dagnell tried hard, and succeeded
finally. He was sleeping peacefully when the
door opened, and Ursula entered. With her
soft, dark dress and noiseless slippers, she
seemed to glide into the room, a ghost-like
figure in the dim light that was there. And it
was the face of a ghost too—cadaverous and
bloodless. The sleeping man in the chair bore a
healthy hue by contrast with her.

Tom's heart gave way a little. No, there
was nothing to tell Ursula Dagnell which she
did not know already. He was sure of it.

CHAPTER X.

THE ENGAGED COUPLE.

ONE very noticeable fact in Ursula Dagnell's appearance was the absence of her glasses —although Tom was not aware of it for some minutes after her entrance. This had rendered her short-sighted, and she came up very closely to Tom, and peered into his face, to make sure it was he.

Her colour did not vary at the sight of him, and her voice was pitched in a low monotone— hardly her voice, Tom thought, and one not swayed by any passion now. It was like a woman's speaking at a distance.

Ursula turned from Tom to her uncle.

" Asleep ?" she inquired.

"Yes," answered Tom; "I could not get him to his bed to-night."

"It matters not," she said. "It is as well he can rest somewhere."

There was a third chair by the fireside, and she took it, leaned her head against the cold marble mantelpiece, and gazed with a fixed intentness at the fire.

"What a stormy night it is," he said.

"Yes. Have you been asleep?"

"No," was the slow answer; "at least I don't think I have."

"Has Sir John complained of my absence?"

"No."

"Has he been sitting there ever since?" she inquired.

Tom did not answer readily.

"He has been a little restless," Tom replied at last; "and he has walked about the room with me."

Singular that he should respond in this evasive way to Ursula—that even in this little matter he must be false to her. It was his father's wish, and for the present he must respect it. He could scarcely mention the name of Violet Hilderbrandt to-night, he thought. And yet he had been waiting long for it—and Ursula knew all. If he could but break the ice, and tell her his version of the story—if he could only say something which would make him look less the traitor he had been, and teach this cousin some gentle lesson of mercy, forbearance, or reconciliation with him!

Was it hopeless?—was it policy to speak to-night?

Ursula closed her eyes, and said—

"You need not remain any longer, Tom."

"You are tired, I am sure."

"What does that matter?" she murmured.

"I shall make a better nurse than you to-night."

"I think not," she replied, wearily, "so please go—now."

Tom rose at her appeal, and she did not open her eyes to see the last of him. He held his hand towards her, but she did not perceive it. He did not stoop and kiss her as he had done last night, by the right of his engagement.

The time was past for him and her—it was all over between these two, who had talked of their everlasting love only a little while ago!

"Good night, Ursula."

"Good night."

As he walked away, some softly whispered words which she had not intended to reach him, came to his quick ears. They were " *God bless you!*" and they thrilled him at that time.

He went back to her side. He stood before her, and called her by her name, but she would not look at him again.

"I came here some hours ago in search of you, Ursula," he murmured in her ears, "I have so much to tell you—to explain. I wanted you——"

"To know all," she added. " Well, I know it. Let me be!"

"Until to-morrow then."

" Ah! yes—to-morrow, please."

"Early to-morrow, if you will come to me in the garden, where there will be no one to interrupt us."

"Where you and I talked once of being man

and wife, I will meet you there," she said in the
same set tones which wavered not, and yet
which had no malice in them. She was speaking of a past without reproach, or passion.

Tom did not understand her, or feared that
he understood her far too well. He said no more,
but went away. She was a woman very weary,
she had been sorely tried; she was "dazed,"
and it would have been ungenerous to confess
his love for Violet that night. She knew it and
had reproached Violet with it, but he had not
spoken himself, he had not the heart.

He went softly along the corridor to his room,
thinking already of the morrow—already preparing for it. As he passed Marcus's door, he
remembered his brother whom he had consoled
at an earlier hour, and the collapse of whose
engagement had so quickly brought about his
own. They were twin brothers in a love which
had shrivelled up in a night. The wax candles
were burning in the room still, under the door a
thin line of light streamed forth across the floor
of the corridor. As he passed, he heard Marcus
cough within.

" Good night, Marcus," he said, tapping on the panels, " you are up too late to-night."

Before he could withdraw, the door was opened, and his brother, as he had seen him last, pale and cravatless, stood in the aperture.

" Oh ! is that you, Tom ? I'm glad you are up. Come in."

" Not now, thank you."

" But I have something to tell you. Look here !"

And Marcus led his brother towards the window, which was still open, and through which the rain was drifting very fast into the room.

CHAPTER XI.

GHOSTS.

WHEN Tom Dagnell was standing with his brother at the open window, there seemed nothing out of the common way to account for Marcus's excitement. The dark expanse of garden ground stretched below them; the trees stood out in inky blackness against the lesser blackness of the sky, and the wind and rain dashed amongst the branches and gave them life and motion in the night.

" Well, what is there to see?" said Tom.

" Do you think any particular shock to a fellow is likely to turn his brain?" asked Marcus.

" What shock have you had?" rejoined Tom.

" Oh! you know—about Fanny."

" That was not a great shock, I hope," said

his brother. "You were to get over it all by
bed-time, if you remember?"

"Ah! yes; that was my bounce, Tom,"
Marcus confessed. "My way of brazening it
out, for I have been awfully floored, 'pon my
soul! But," putting his glass to his eye, and
peering down carefully into the garden. "It
didn't strike me, I had gone out of my mind
until a little while ago. Do you see anything in
the garden at all? Anything wrong!"

"No."

"No more do I," said Marcus.

"Why then——"

"But I have seen a great deal," he went on;
"the whole place below there has been haunted,
or else my brain's really gone, 'pon honour."

"What have you seen?"

"People moving about down there, just as if
it were summer time, and there was a garden
party on," replied Marcus. "I could have
sworn Ursula was in the garden an hour or two
ago, or a woman of some sort that looked like
her. But then you see she was with the
governor."

"Yes, that settles the delusion," answered Tom, in a low tone.

"Besides, Ursula does not walk about in the rain and toss her arms to and fro, like a wretched lunatic."

"No, that is not like Ursula," said Tom. "Did you call to her?"

"Call!" replied Marcus, "with my tongue like a plaster of Paris cast in my mouth? I was too scared, Tom, by Jove!"

"Did she see you at the window?" Tom inquired.

"Don't think she did," was the reply; "and yet she looked round. Do ghosts look over their shoulder, Tom?"

"I can't say," replied his brother. "Well, what else?"

"Then there has been a man, or the ghost of one, in a hat too big for him, muddling about, too," Marcus continued. "I called to that, and it went on under the verandah, and disappeared."

"You have had a lively night of it," Tom remarked.

" That's not all."

" Well ?"

" Well," repeated his brother, " a little while ago back came the woman, or the ghost of the woman—or another woman—over the lawn, dragging herself along by the trees and the garden seats, as if it were hard work to get on —not a bit like Ursula now! So that shows I was wrong—or queer, or something."

" What was the woman like?"

" I can't tell you. She'll catch an awful cold presently, for she had nothing on her head, and her hair was all down her back and over her face; and she did not seem able to find her way for it. Not that hair would make any difference to an apparition, I suppose."

" Why did you not leap down and stop her?" said Tom; "ask who she was, and what she wanted ?"

" Ye—es, not a bad idea," was Marcus's slow remark, "only it's fourteen feet down, and I might have snapped myself in half. Besides, I'm not brave, Tom, and I had not the pluck."

"It is singular," muttered Tom, "unless you have been dreaming."

"I called out at last 'Who's there?' but nobody answered," said Marcus. "And then that stupid animal Cab turned up, and I shouted to him to stop her. I shall have a fine sore throat in the morning, I expect, with all this bawling."

"The dog was there, then?" asked Tom.

"Upon my word, I'm not quite sure it wasn't the ghost of a dog too," Marcus replied, "for it crawled on like a snake, and deuce a bit of notice did it take of me, but followed the woman, or the ghost, and disappeared."

"You should have come to me," said Tom, angrily; "you were quick enough to knock me up at Elmslie House when the thieves broke in."

"Don't remind me of Birmingham, please," entreated Marcus, "I can't bear any more of that."

"I beg your pardon," said Tom. "Never mind me, Marcus."

"Besides—I was fixed here—I expected

somebody else. I have been waiting ever since
for the next movement," Marcus continued, " it
did not seem the end of it. I fancied Fanny
would appear. I thought something had happened to her."

" Shut the window, Marcus, there will be no
more ghosts to-night," said Tom, mournfully.

" How do you know? How——"

" It may be easily explained—it may remain
a mystery for ever," said his brother. "I have
a wild idea which I dare not trouble you
with—for I may be awfully in the wrong about
it."

Marcus shut the window.

" Some of the servants are up to their larks,
perhaps," said Marcus. " We have an odd lot
of them in this house. You don't believe in
apparitions ?"

" No."

" I haven't been so alarmed for years—never
in my life, in fact," said Marcus. "I hope all
this will not make me ill."

" It will do you good," said Tom.

"Will it, by gad?" exclaimed Marcus, in amazement.

"It has prevented your brooding too much on Fanny—and I had left you in a bad way, old boy. It has distracted you—been a change—and the ghost of the old love has not sat so close to your heart. Only those ghosts outside!"

Tom was excited himself, and spoke with passion. If he were near the solution to the mystery, it had scared him with its ghastly horror—unperceived even by him who had drawn attention to it. Was Tom Dagnell in spirit-land, and already haunted, that he looked so miserably beset?

"You don't think there is occasion to watch any longer?" Marcus asked.

"No. The play's over," Tom said, scoffingly, " and the——"

He did not complete his sentence; both young men looked vaguely at each other, and the colour of each changed despite their apprenticeship to the mysterious. There was a scratching of nails against the door—startling enough at that hour, and with their nerves highly strung—and then the low long whine of Cab re-assured them, and told them that the dog was still wandering about the corridor, as if loth to leave his master.

"Cab will wake the house," said Tom, advancing to the door.

"They say dogs see spirits, don't they?" asked Marcus, who was fairly upset that evening.

"Ay, and give warnings too," was the reply, as Tom opened the door and Cab came whining into the room, with the same difficulty, dragging his limbs after him, and panting hard as he approached his master.

"My poor old Cab," said Tom, dropping down on his knees beside him, "I wish you could tell me what is the matter, what misery and trouble have been abroad with you to-night? You would tell me if you could. You —Oh! Marcus, look here! He's dying!"

Yes, poor Cab had dragged himself to his young master's feet to die; he had struggled upstairs once more for a last look of the kindly face, a last caress of the strong friendly hand.

Cab had been bleeding slowly to death for some time, and this was the end of it. He had met his death-blow on that night, and there was no one to tell them how this faithful servant had come by his end.

It was only a dog's death, but there were tears in Tom Dagnell's eyes as he bent over the faithful servant he had lost.

CHAPTER XII.

NEXT MORNING.

THERE had been no time mentioned for Tom
Dagnell's interview with his cousin; it
was to be early in the morning, in the garden
where she had first warned him of his father's
wish for their marriage. He was astir early
in consequence; it was necessary to be wakeful
in these new days, wherein there was much
plotting, and where strange events were
happening hourly. There was much for Ursula
Dagnell to explain, he thought, after the
humiliation of his own confession had been
fought through and succumbed to. He did not
dream that the time for explanation was not
yet, and that Ursula and he were to meet again

under circumstances stranger than these. He
had rehearsed his miserable part all the weary
time before daylight; he had prepared his
story and set it, as he hoped, in its best light;
he did not wholly despair, vain dreamer, of
interesting Ursula in his love for Violet Hilderbrandt. For Ursula was an honest woman,
and full of wondrous impulses of self-sacrifice,
and the times were ripe for them again. What
would not a woman do for love's sake? What
would he not have done himself to make
Ursula happy and free, if——. Then his reason-
ing became clouded; and the mist of his own
fancies, perhaps of his illusions, gathered thick-
ly round him. He was looking forward to self-
sacrifice on her part; he could not believe in
the good of self-sacrifice on his, though he
might be prepared for it. That would make
no one happy, he was sure; that would be un-
natural and base from the beginning to the
end. On the other hand, a few kind words, a
few regretful tears, and then happiness all
round, like a finis to a pleasant story-book.

It was eight in the morning when Tom Dag-

nell was in the breakfast-room, biding his time
as patiently as he could, and keeping his gaze
directed to the garden lying beyond the windows. The rain, which had fallen heavily
last night, had not ceased; it was a steady
down-pour from the sullen clouds hanging over
Broadlands. It was altogether an ill time for
a lover's tryst in the free air—even for such
despairing lovers as he and Ursula. and with
such a fate before them.

Tom stood at the window and watched the
rain-drops on the glass. Ursula would keep
her appointment; she was a woman of her
word; she would send for him presently; perhaps come to him where he was—in all her
life she had been precise to a degree, and there
would be no fear of facing him at last, at the
bitter last, like this!

There was no one moving in the house of
whom he could ask questions; the inmates were
late astir that day, as if to balk him. The feet
of one or two lazy servants shuffled without,
but there was no one of his own family to greet
him, and Violet, always an early riser, was still

absent, was probably holding herself aloof from him after last night's parting, which he would have taken to his aching heart as final, had she not promised to remain at Broadlands.

Still he did not expect to see Violet Hilderbrandt; he hardly dreamed of meeting her; he felt all was changed between them, and that this was a cruel intermediate state to be ended in one way or another, before the day was done, thank Heaven!

His mother had taken to early rising lately, but she was not down that morning; Marcus remained in his room; there were no news from the upstairs domain where Sir John fought for his life, and Ursula reigned supreme; even garrulous Robin Fisher was digging poor Cab's grave out in the damp plantation, by order of his master.

Tom breakfasted alone; he had grown so accustomed to his loneliness that the sudden opening of the door made him start. It was not Ursula, or Violet, however; it was only Mrs. Coombes, bland and business-like as usual, with her hands crossed on her black silk apron.

"I beg your pardon, Mr. Dagnell, but I thought her ladyship was here," she said, half backing from the room again.

"One word. How is Sir John this morning?" asked Tom.

"About the same, sir. He is sleeping very soundly now."

"And Miss Dagnell. Is she with him?"

Mrs. Coombes looked surprised, even discomfited, by the question, and Tom, who seemed ever on the alert, was quick to note the change in her.

"Where is Miss Dagnell?" he said, sharply.

"Well, sir, I was not to tell you yet awhile—and that is the plain truth," Mrs. Coombes confessed. "Miss Dagnell thought it might alarm you perhaps, and——"

"Go on. What is the matter?"

"If you please, sir, you will not say I told you," said Mrs. Coombes; "I don't care to make words, and Miss Ursula can be very hard upon me for disobeying orders—no one harder."

"Why don't you explain?" cried Tom, impatiently.

"Miss Dagnell was taken ill suddenly, sir, and rang for me about half-past four or five to sit up with Sir John. She's in her bed, very weak and faint, and wants to see her ladyship."

"Has anyone sent for a doctor?"

"She will not have a doctor," was the reply. "She will be downstairs presently, she says— but, oh! dear, she looks very dreadful, to be sure. So grey-like!"

"Did she say I was not to know this?"

"Yes, Mr. Dagnell," answered Mrs. Coombes, "that is what she is particularly anxious about, at present. 'If he asks for me,' she said, 'don't tell him I am ill. Under any circumstances, don't tell him I am ill.'"

"Strange," muttered Tom Dagnell.

"She said something about twelve o'clock, too," continued Mrs. Coombes. "'Tell him twelve o'clock, if he should ask for me; and that I'm very busy till then. But don't see him, if it's possible—don't speak a word, if you can help it,' she kept on saying till I left her."

"Let a doctor be sent for immediately."

" Yes, sir," replied Mrs. Coombes, " but Miss Dagnell says she will not have a doctor."

" Go to Lady Dagnell's room at once."

" Yes, sir."

" And to Miss Hilderbrandt's, and——"

" Oh! I was not to tell her, if you please, sir," said Mrs. Coombes. " Oh! dear no, she was not to know of this. Miss Ursula flew into a terrible passion when I said Miss Hilderbrandt would be the one to send for. It's her temper which frightens me, and makes me think she has broken down at last with over-anxiety about Sir John."

" Find out her ladyship—tell her I am waiting here, after she has seen her niece. Why don't you go?" said Tom.

Mrs. Coombes was only too glad to escape, and hastened to shut Tom in with his own thoughts, which were many and disturbing, which belonged to last night's work, and the new fears of the morning, and were inextricably involved. It seemed impossible that he should know all before the day was over; and yet Violet had promised him, and

even Sir John and Ursula had intimated the
same, as if they were conscious that he hated
mystery, and were anxious to dispel the clouds
around him. Could they explain all, though;
was it in their power, or did there lie a mystery
beyond them to which no solution was possible?
Did they know of Marcus's haunted hours in
his own room, and were they wild fragments of
the secret also? With the sky darkening
before him, and the rain hissing like a snake, he
sat there and thought that he was farther from
the light than ever. Presently his mother
entered in her dressing-gown, and sank into a
chair, weak and prostrate.

"As if there were not trouble enough for us
without this," she moaned.

"Is Ursula very ill?" asked Tom, anxiously.

"Yes, she is very ill," said Lady Dagnell,
"and very obstinate."

"Have you sent for advice?"

"She will wait until Dr. Smiles calls to see
Sir John," replied Lady Dagnell; "she wants
nothing but rest, she says. Rest and peace of
mind, as if there were any to be got in this house!"

"Ursula has broken down with fatigue; she has been over-worked," said Tom; "no one has helped her fairly."

"If that is a hit off at your mother, I can bear it," said Lady Dagnell, languidly, "although it is not fatigue which has prostrated Ursula. Oh! dear no."

"What is it?"

"Bad temper—jealousy, or something of the kind; and I'm not surprised at it. I have seen this coming on a long while; and," added Lady Dagnell, "been glad of it too! She was never fit for you, Thomas; you should have known that long ago."

"I am not fit for her, you mean." replied Tom, moodily.

"An exacting, domineering, over-righteous young woman—a——"

"That will do, mother."

"Do you know she has told Violet Hilderbrandt to quit the house to-day, and that she will not leave her own room until Violet has gone. There, that's the illness of your Ursula, if you must know," she said, vindictively.

" When Violet has left Broadlands, Miss Dagnell will condescend to be with the family again— not before."

" Has she told you this?"

" She has."

" I must see her," said Tom, springing to his feet. " I will see Ursula immediately."

" She is too ill for that," replied Lady Dagnell, somewhat alarmed now. " She is quite ill enough for the doctor, in fact. I have sent for him on my own responsibility."

" That is good," said Tom. " And—Violet?"

" She is in her own room."

" You have seen her. She is well?"

" Yes."

" And preparing to leave us. My God! going away into her dangerous world again," moaned Tom.

" I don't know," said Lady Dagnell. " I hardly think so. There are no boxes packed; she is calm and grave and unexcited. She is waiting, she says."

" Ah! for me," cried Tom. " Remind her of her promise not to leave in haste, and until I have seen Ursula myself at mid-day. Tell Violet all may change from that hour, and all be well."

He passed from the room into the hall, where a servant was admitting a tall, ill-clad lad, who was slipping sideways past the door, and glancing askance at the domestic during the operation. The quick, restless eyes of the intruder caught sight of Tom, and the lad ran to him with a sharp yelp of delight.

" Why, you're the werry bloke I wants," he screamed. " Here, come out of this, will yer? or put me somewhere where I can patter to yer. Don't yer know me?"

" Larry Simes !" exclaimed our hero. " What do you want? Is your master here—or any of your gang ?"

" No sich luck," was the reply. " That's the wust o' it—that's the orfullest wust of it, yer see."

" What do you want?"

" Can't yer guess wot I'm here for—wot lay I've been on all these blessed weeks ?" cried Larry. " Oh, yer are a cove, s'elp me !"

"Come out with me, boy."

"All right. Where's your dawg? Don't bring *him*."

"No, I'll not."

"All right agin. And how is the dawg?"

"Dead."

"Is he really? Poor dawg now."

Tom seized his hat, and went into the rain, followed by Larry Simes, who, though limping sorely, managed to keep up with him by breaking into a run occasionally. Tom led the way to the sea-shore, as if it were a fitting place for their interview, and less a scandal to him.

He could not trust those in his own house, which was full of eavesdroppers, and this concerned Violet Hilderbrandt, and perhaps her safety. Or it might be the beginning of the end of this hateful mystery, and in some way applicable to all that had happened last night. Or it might be danger to Violet or himself; this boy was a stormy petrel, and had always preceded the storm and the wreck.

CHAPTER XIII.

THE WARNING.

THE rain had subsided in a great degree, but the wind had gathered strength, and was at its worst upon the coast line. It came at them fiercely as they passed from the cutting to the sands, and both man and boy struggled against it, and turned their faces from it, whilst it rushed screaming by them, carrying along a never-ceasing drift of sand, and tangled weeds, and sea spray. The tide was rising, and the great green waves broke with thunderous bellowings on the shore. It was a wild day out at sea, and there were foam and fury in the waters and under the dull, dead sky.

"Gord's truth!" exclaimed the boy, his favourite exclamation escaping him as he clutched at his cap, and his ragged fringes fluttered in the breeze, "this is a place to bring a cove, and no flies! And as if I hadn't eno' o' it last night."

"Last night?"

"Oh! never mind—wot's the odds?"

"We are safe here," said Tom; "you can tell me everything now."

"Wait till I get breath, then," said Larry, shivering very violently.

Tom waited, and the lad said, at last—

"It's all up. The gal must cut. They're comin' to the 'ouse to-day."

"Who—who are coming?"

"The slops—coppers—bobbies, yer fool," said Larry, unceremoniously and rudely.

"The police are coming to Broadlands—after——"

"The guv'nor's gal. She's to be took to-day."

"Who told you this? How have you discovered it?" asked Tom.

"Oh, I ain't been about for nuffink," said

Larry, conceitedly. "I've been hanging round Little'ampton—all my 'spenses paid, too—to make sure there wasn't no artful kid on, as the guv'nor thought, yer twig? Don't yer twig?" asked Larry, as Tom's face expressed still more astonishment.

"I do not guess anything yet," replied our hero.

"I was to let him know when anythink was up," said Larry, "and I've had by me weeks, one of them things yer sends by telly-grasp for him to get as quick as winkin', and he's got it, and can't come—and I was to run to yer crib—and yer not likely to split—and yer'll get the gal away for us, won't yer now? Say s'elp yer gord, and wish yer may die, and I'll b'leeve yer, old 'un."

"Yes, yes, she must be saved," said Tom; "her father may trust me to do my best for her. Where is her father?"

"That's more than any on us know," replied Larry. "He's werry much out o' the way, and werry careful of hisself at present. So's old Jardine—so's bandy Moke—so's the Spider, the

Brummagem Spider, I mean, who was nigh nobbled about Oliver's crib—your pal."

"What!" exclaimed Tom.

"Oh, ah, yer innercent, and live in a big 'ouse—I forgot," said Larry, with bitter irony; "and yer didn't crack Oliver's along with the Spider and go 'alves, and leave me out of it, and not a blooming tanner of the swag for Larry—oh, no! He wasn't good enuf for that fakement; yer leave him the barrers and the aireys, and he's a'most had enough on 'em, he has."

"I must get home," said Tom; "I have no time to reason with you. You are of a world where all men are thieves. Can't you get away from it, poor devil?"

"Yer aint comin' a preachin' lay, are yer?" asked Larry, with considerable astonishment and fear; "yer *have* been one o' us, 'aven't yer?"

"God forbid!"

"Then why——"

"I must return. Every minute is valuable, if you have told me the truth," said Tom

"Here, boy, is that any good to you? Will it keep you from stealing for a day or two? It is all I have in my pocket."

Larry's fingers closed upon the sovereign which Tom dropped into his hand, opened again to allow of a proper facility for spitting on the coin for good luck, then closed finally and tightly.

"Thankee," muttered Larry. "That's like a real gemman, that is!"

"And now be off, and grow honest if you can. Run away to sea, Larry, and drop the whole lot of them. Run anywhere, you'll find better luck than this."

"To sea! What, that beastly stuff over there!" yelled Larry, pointing to the ocean. "No, no, guv'nor, not me!"

Tom heard him, but did not stop to continue his homily. He was full of anxiety and excitement; of all the cares to which he had looked forward—home cares, home troubles, troubles with Ursula and Violet—this had not been foreshadowed or prepared for. This had receded into the background—seemed to belong to a past which they had all outlived—and which, rising up suddenly and ghastly in their midst, only assured him what a little while it was ago!

With his head bowed against the wind and sleet, he went on as towards a fate which it was difficult to fight against—which seemed like the storm to press him back. The shadows were deepening around him, the danger was closer at hand than it had ever been, and he more powerless to act. Yes, he was sure, more powerless! For Violet Hilderbrandt was working against him, and would not have his help. He knew it; he was sure of it; her words of yesterday were ringing in his ears; looks and signs of yesterday were before his mental vision, and were as proofs of holy writ, which there was no disregarding.

One mystery was clearing up before him; the light of day—a cold, clear, awful light— was on it, and the waif he had left behind on the sands, in all his ignorance and squalor, had been wise enough to give the clue.

Violet Hilderbrandt knew of her danger last night, and was prepared for it. She had bidden him farewell for ever on the threshold of his father's room. She had seen already the terrible coming of this day, and had given up all hope concerning it. Hilderbrandt had probably communicated with her, to put her on her guard—and had only given her strength to meet the trial bravely, instead of eluding it as she had done before. Tom knew what she would do and say—he could prophesy her future actions, and her defiance of his wishes. He knew too well that he was running madly homewards in vain to her rescue, and that the time for him to act was gone. She would be truer to Ursula than to him—she would prove to Ursula how strong, and brave and unselfish a girl she was—and Ursula would let her prove it. Unless,—ah! unless Ursula was merciful, and would of her own free will say to him, "Go to her. She is the woman you love best. I give you up." Ursula was strong, and brave and unselfish too; no woman in the world had acted more generously than she had, once in her strange life. And she would do more for him, he thought. It would be right to take counsel of Ursula—if Ursula were only well!

He was standing in the hall of his father's house at last; he had run all the way, but the distance had never seemed so long, or such an uphill toil, from the sea shore to Broadlands. The servant who admitted him, stared with surprise at his flushed and excited face, and when Tom gasped forth, "Where is Miss Hilderbrandt?" it was in so stern a tone that he went back a step or two in his dismay.

"Miss Hilderbrandt, sir, has gone out with Mr. Marcus," he stammered forth.

"With Marcus!" shouted Tom. "Miss Hilderbrandt has gone out with my brother?"

"Yes, sir, in the carriage. I saw them."

"Which way?"

The servant was giving his directions when Lady Dagnell opened the drawing-room door, and came into the hall. The loud tone of her son's voice had apprised her of his return, and she had been waiting for him very anxiously.

"Oh! dear," she said, "why did you leave

the house at such an awful time as this?"

"Why has Violet gone away?" he cried.

"My dear son, I couldn't stop her."

"She promised me she——"

"Yes, yes; Ursula will explain all."

"But Ursula is——"

"She is in the drawing-room. She is waiting for you."

CHAPTER XIV.

THE STORM BURSTS.

THERE was no time lost in discussing the question with Lady Dagnell. The last words had hardly escaped the mother's lips when her son was in the drawing-room, fierce and impetuous, a figure from the old days, protesting against his injuries.

"Where is Violet?" he exclaimed. "Why has she gone away? Who has the right in this house to bid her go, without consulting me? Who——"

He had forgotten Ursula's illness, but his voice failed him and his passion subsided at the sight of his cousin. Here was a woman injured by his breach of faith and want of love, and suffering very much. The agony, compressed and acute, upon her face would have silenced harder men than he—it told so complete a story of utter hopelessness.

Ursula sat in an arm-chair by the window; she was propped up by many cushions, and looked like one who had been carried downstairs to die. The daylight, which was strong upon her, brought into relief strange lines and furrows, and deep dark shadows underneath the eyes, from which the glasses were still absent. Ten years seemed to have passed over her since they had met last—ten years of bodily and mental pain.

" Ursula, I am sorry you are ill," Tom exclaimed, in a different voice. " I am harsh and forgetful, and selfish. But see how I have been tried !"

" We all have our crosses to bear," said Ursula, in a low voice. " It has come to me as well as you."

" My mother tells me you will explain this; but are you strong enough ?" he asked. " Is it worth the risk ?"

"I am here to explain," was the reply.

"I will not listen now—I will not harass you," said Tom, hurriedly; "to-morrow, the next day, weeks hence, when you are stronger. Only tell me where Violet is, where I can find her, just to say good-bye to her!"

The grave face into which he was gazing quivered suddenly at his earnestness, at the love for another which he betrayed, but the voice which responded to him was without a wavering note.

"She has left for Honfleur by the Littlehampton steamer," Ursula replied.

"Gone! Left England!—and without a word to me," cried Tom. "Why was I not consulted? Why have I been treated thus unfairly? Oh! Ursula, did you advise her to go away like this?"

"I have offered no advice," was the answer. "She has left Broadlands of her own free will. I have not said a word to her to-day."

"You told her yesterday to go."

"Ah! yesterday," moaned Ursula; "it is a long while since yesterday."

"You ordered her from the house, as if the house were yours," he said, more warmly.

"It will be mine upon your father's death—and that may be to-morrow," Ursula replied.

"The house yours!—but there, there, I do not care who has it—I do not care what becomes of it, or me, or anything—only of that poor hunted girl."

"I am not hunting her, and you need not reprove me," said Ursula. "Yesterday I reminded her of a past contract between us, that was all. When I doubted her, she was to go away; and she has gone, thank God!"

The grey eyes regarded her lover unflinchingly, and there was a lurid glow in them which spoke of much power to resist still. He had not thought of Ursula's feelings in all this, and of what she had suffered, for it to come to this; he was thinking only of Violet Hilderbrandt, and Ursula's heart grew hard and cold.

"I may be able to overtake her yet," Tom said, full of a new impulse, "and here I waste time and——"

"The steamer has left the harbour," Ursula

remarked; "I saw it from the window of my room put out to sea. I have been waiting for it to go."

"Is there no note—no message for me?"

"You can ask Marcus when he returns from the quay," was Ursula's reply. "It is no business of mine."

"Did you send her back to Honfleur?"

"I did not care which way she went, so that it was from Broadlands," said Ursula.

"Why has she gone to France?"

"She has told your mother that."

Tom turned quickly, but Lady Dagnell was not in the room. She had a horror of scenes that might excite her nerves or depress them, and she had deemed it politic to leave Tom and Ursula to themselves.

"But you know," persisted Tom. "And— Ursula, you *must* tell me."

"I thought you were going to spare me—to postpone all this till I was well," she answered, bitterly. "Do you think I am quite strong enough to bear it?"

"Forgive me if I am inconsiderate," said Tom

again, "but Violet came here at our wish, and we have driven her away."

"*We* have!" muttered Ursula.

"I have so much to say in my defence," said Tom, "so much to explain and to ask your pardon for, Ursula, and, in sparing you, I must look base and ungrateful for a while. But— you know!"

"Yes; I know," was the hollow response again.

"Tell me of Violet, and of her sudden journey," urged Tom. "For Heaven's sake, say something! You have had your way; will not that suffice?"

Ursula did not answer readily. For a moment it seemed as if she had not the strength to speak, and that the thin lips were moving vainly, but the reply came at length.

"I am not in Miss Hilderbrandt's confidence," she said. "I know little of what has happened during the last twelve hours, save that she received a letter late last night from her father— the man who trades in stolen goods."

"Who told you she received a letter?"

Ursula went on without replying to his question.

"It was a warning of danger from other hands than mine," Ursula continued, gloomily. "She had been traced, and the police were likely to arrest her in this house. To save us that disgrace she left us hurriedly."

"She will not escape by going to France. She——"

He stopped, there was so ghastly a smile upon the worn face before him.

"Can you laugh at all this misery? You!" he cried, indignantly, again.

"I am smiling at your conjectures, which are wide of the truth, and deceive you," she replied, in the same measured tones. "She will not escape. She does not go to France to escape, but to deliver herself up!"

"Good God!"

"This is a heroine whom you worship, Mr. Dagnell, and not a weak creature full of faults and failings, mean jealousies, and petty spites, as are most women by whose acquaintance you have been afflicted." Ursula went on more coldly, if it were possible. "She is innocent, and will bear the shame no longer of being considered guilty, she says. She is a perfect heroine, and deserving of every good man's sympathy; she had a right to take your love from me, if not to take the diamonds. What am I but the villain of this story?"

Tom approached her again, and would have spoken, but her next words stopped him.

"But," she continued, triumphantly, "you will never see her again. She is beyond you. The prison walls will be between you two, and I am very glad of it."

"Ursula," cried Tom, losing his self-command once more, and forgetting all but Violet's tribulation, "as God's my judge, I believe you have betrayed her!"

His voice rang through the room with a trumpet-sound, and for the first time dismayed his listener, or else his flushed face and blazing eyes told of his sudden hate of her, and struck deep into her heart. She cowered in her chair, as if afraid of him, and with a quick movement she wheeled herself some little distance back, as though a fear that he might strike her had possessed her.

"You think," she gasped forth, "so bad of me as that?"

"You were away last night from my father," he continued—"from the house which you left to bear false witness against Violet. Marcus saw you in the garden—it is all as clear as day to me!"

"No, no, NO!" screamed Ursula, and she stood up as if she were well and strong again; 'it is not true, you dare not think it of me—you are not such a dastard. You must unsay that—you must unsay that, Tom Dagnell, if you please!"

She held her arms out and tottered towards him; she would have fallen, if he had not caught her and led her back to her chair, into which she sank with a feeble cry.

"I will say no more now," said Tom; "I forget myself. I will send some one to you."

"But you believe it," she replied, clinging to his sleeve with both her hands, "and some one

has poisoned your mind against me. You *have*
seen her, after all."

"You left the house last night," said Tom;
"you were seen in the garden by Marcus. I
have no more to say now, Ursula, save Heaven
forgive you!"

Again she was standing up before him, with
her arms outstretched, as if appealing for his
mercy or his better judgment.

"Tom, I—I left the house only to die!" she
cried. "I was sick of life when I had lost you,
and I went away to end it. I could not live
without you, and I preferred to go!"

"And you——"

"I went down to the sea and plunged in for
rest. I wanted only to die, and they would not
let me!"

"They?"

"They brought me to shore—the dog, the
dreadful dog, and some one who had been
watching me—and I came home more than
half dead at last—came back to life for this—
oh, my good God, for this!"

She sank back in her chair with an awful

scream, which was heard throughout the house and brought the servants in with blanched cheeks and trembling limbs—which startled Sir John Dagnell dozing before the fire, and caused him to sit up and listen attentively—which scared Lady Dagnell into hysterics, and much especial attention to herself.

"I have killed her!" cried Tom, "see to her, some of you women. Send for the doctor again—do something. Ursula, it is all my own fault, I have been wrong to judge you—forgive me! Don't you hear me, Ursula?"

But though the eyes were unclosed they did not look at him, and from the parted lips issued no further sound. She was struck into stone, and they bore her to her room, very silent and uncomplaining now, with the semblance of death so strong upon her that the whisper went through Broadlands that Ursula Dagnell had, by God's awful visitation, passed away before the master.

CHAPTER XV.

RESOLUTIONS.

DESPITE all his thought and all his love for Violet Hilderbrandt, it had been Tom Dagnell's fate to be never of any service to her. His mission to Birmingham had been a failure, and had only involved him in difficulties, and now, at this great crisis of her life, he was once more completely helpless. Once again had the bitter thought come to him that here was a woman in danger and he powerless to assist her—as he had always been, as though a spell were resting on him in times of grave emergency.

Violet Hilderbrandt was beyond his friendly care; there was no hurrying to her rescue. The

Littlehampton steamer had put forth boldly in the face of the storm, and carried her away from him. Under no circumstances was it in his power to reach her now, to beg her to recon- sider the importance of the step which she had taken, and which would for ever influence her life.. She had grown weary of hiding like a criminal, and had resolved to confront her accusers and bear the brunt of the battle, come what would. And she had passed suddenly from Broadlands, so that on English ground and in English courts of law her name should not be connected with those who had been kind to her.

There was still something to explain, Tom thought; the light of day was not upon the motives of them all, and the wheels of the gods, grinding slowly all his hopes to powder, con- tained many inner wheels which were worth the studying. He was near the truth, and he would find it shortly. Who had warned Violet Hilder- brandt of her danger of arrest at Broadlands, and when? Whether that warning was the one good action of his father's last night, and the reason why Violet had kissed him, the son, in sign of eternal separation? If so, who had warned Sir John, and how had the warning reached him in the sick-room, when the spy, Larry, told off for the purpose, knew nothing till the following day? All this had to be pieced out to the end, and he was close upon the end, he thought.. It was the termination of a sad journey, with the red sun sinking ominously amidst the ruins of his life, and of more lives than his.

It was remarkable all these thoughts should be possessing him in the midst of that anxiety for Ursula Dagnell which he could but experience after her confession; that they should take the foremost place, even at that hour, and set her illness and despair in the background as a something appertaining to the mystery, but to be thought of more intently at a future time. Friends came downstairs to inform him Ursula was better and conscious, and the doctor thought she would soon be well again, with care; and he answered he was glad to hear it, with the same gloomy cast of countenance, and with the same pre-occupied gaze

which had been with him all the morning. He
was acutely pained that he had misjudged his
cousin, and that in her despair at losing him
she had sought to end her life. He had been
conscience-stricken by her accusation of his
breach of faith ; but still for ever foremost, and
not to be set aside, were his despairing thoughts
of Violet, and his wild conjectures as to what
would be the result of her rash step. Presently
Ursula, and his father, and the intricate net-
work of lines crossing and re-crossing their
mysterious lives, should have his .earnest
thought ; but the time was now for Violet, and
in what way he could prove how he was plotting, struggling, sorrowing for her.

When Marcus returned in the carriage, it
was his brother Tom who opened the door for
him, and hurled at him question after question
peremptorily, until all that Marcus could im-
part to him in the way of information had been
elicited by fierce cross-questioning.

There was not a great deal to announce, and
Tom had guessed most of it already. Violet
had started by *The Witch*—the same unlucky

steamer which had brought her first to England—for Honfleur; there had been grave doubts of the vessel leaving in so rough a sea, but the order had been given for departure, and Marcus had taken his farewell of Violet Hilderbrandt, and seen the vessel steam out of the harbour.

She had told him part of her story, and of the dangers which had been threatening her, but not a word of Ursula or Sir John had escaped her lips. She had spoken of her impulse to face the truth, and end uncertainty for ever, and she had not forgotten a last message to his brother.

"Tell Tom he will render me his debtor by remaining passive in this matter; he cannot help me, and I pray he will not attempt it," she had said. "I leave the end of this to my God, for the end has come!"

"Yes, it is the end," groaned Tom, "but I will see it, for all that. Does she think I am to remain here, and take no further interest in her? Is that like me?"

"There's not much chance of doing anything,

that I can see," replied Marcus, "and you had better keep quiet until we get some news."

" Will she give herself up at Honfleur, do you think ?"

" By gad, she has arranged that. She's wonderfully plucky," replied Marcus. " She has even sent a message to the French police with the information of what she intends to do."

" She is mad to throw away her liberty," said Tom. " But we must be prepared. Counsel shall defend her, and do their best to save her, even against herself. How can I get to France to-day, I wonder ?"

" I thought I told you it was her wish you should not——"

" Yes," said Tom, interrupting him, " but I cannot regard a wish like that."

" You will not leave Broadlands ?"

" Why not ?"

" With Ursula ill—with the governor deprived of her care—with——"

" What are they to me ?" exclaimed Tom, fiercely. " Have they been friends of hers ?

Have I been a friend to them? Can I do any good here?"

"Can you do any good abroad?" replied Marcus—"at all events, till we know the up-shot of this step. By gad, I don't think so."

"She is alone in the world, and utterly friendless."

"No; there you mistake," replied Marcus. "Didn't I tell you Mr. and Mrs. Slitherwick were on board, going that way to France? I have seen Fanny after all, and offered her my congratulations, and I have shaken hands with Slitherwick."

"You are of a forgiving nature."

"You might have knocked me down with a feather when I saw them and their boxes on the quay," said Marcus; "but I was, 'pon my soul, Tom, quite courageous—quite magnanimous. You should have seen me."

"Ah! I wish I had been there," said Tom, with a sigh; "but she left me without a word."

"What! Fanny did?"

"No; Violet, you ass!"

"Oh! she did not intend that, but you had gone out of the house."

"And it was not planned to get me from it, then?" said Tom.

"Planned?" exclaimed Marcus.

"No, no; it is I who am unjust, not she," cried Tom, "I who am eternally suspicious. But she is with Fanny and her husband. They will be of help to her—and I am very glad of that. These Slitherwicks will be her friends—they will communicate with us, and let us know the result of her arrival at Honfleur; we shall not be left wholly in the dark. You have asked them to do their best in her interest, and until I can reach Paris? You have told them to spare no expense in securing the best advice—to call on the prosecutor, and explain how impossible it is that she should be an accomplice in this crime—to write with every post to us, and leave not a stone unturned to be of help to her."

"Ye-es, exactly, I'm sure they will do all that," answered Marcus, staggering beneath this weight of question and suggestion, "and

Fanny will let us know immediately she reaches
Honfleur, or Slitherwick will, unless he's too
sick. I left him getting very green to begin
with. I would not have gone out in that ship
myself for any money," he added, with a per-
ceptible quivering of his spine. "Poor Fanny,
too, she'll be awfully queer. She never could
stand a row-boat."

"It is fortunate they are with Violet," said
Tom, thoughtfully; "but there is no trusting
them with the responsibility of her safety. How
can I get away to-day?"

"Why, you don't think, after all, of——"

"I shall make one more maniac in this house,
if I remain," cried Tom. "Marcus, I will go!"

Man disposes! But it was destined other-
wise, and Tom Dagnell was bound down per-
force to Broadlands, as to a prison, from which
he was not to break free. The torrent of
events was running swiftly its course. There
was no resisting it, and our hero was swept
along in its current, despite the strength of his
resolves, and the power of the love that was in
him.

It was as well he had not his own way, though he grieved long at his own utter uselessness. But then Tom Dagnell was one of life's unfortunates, and had never known what was best.

CHAPTER XVI.

MORE QUESTIONS.

THE next hour of Tom Dagnell's existence was spent in tracing out his journey, and in studying various ways by which he could leave England, and turn his back upon an unlucky house. When he had decided that the most expeditious route, after all, would be to start for London, and then book for the Continent, *via* Dover and Calais, and when he had begun to pack his portmanteau, and to regard his mission as finally resolved upon, there came the doctor, like a black messenger of Fate, to thwart him if he could.

"Your father is not so well to-day, Mr. Dagnell," was the information given.

"It is not likely he would be," answered Tom.

"I think there is a change for the worse."

"He will change for the better to-morrow," was the hard reply.

"I fear not."

Tom looked up from his portmanteau, which lay open in the middle of the room into which Dr. Smiles had been shown.

"Is there a grave change, then?" he inquired, anxiously, "or is this the natural result of a restless night? He left his room last night, and walked along the corridor with Fisher, the butler."

"It was unwise," replied the doctor, "but I am uncertain if it has done him any material harm. Still, Mr. Dagnell, he must not be left to-day on any account."

"I have to start for Paris, on urgent private business," muttered our hero. "And I must go at once."

"Let me advise you to remain," said the doctor, very earnestly. "This is a house in which serious distress, mental and bodily, exists, and you may be the only one of service to allay it."

" I do not comprehend," said Tom.

"Your father and your cousin Ursula are both very ill," continued the doctor.

"I can do them no good," was the old stubborn answer.

" On the contrary, you may do a great deal of good, by not deserting them."

" There is my brother Marcus; there is my mother," said Tom. " Did I not tell you there was pressing business demanding my immediate departure ?"

" Mr. Dagnell," said the old gentleman, "it would be idle for me to disguise the fact that I know you have not been good friends with your father; but I think, at such a time as this, all enmity should cease."

" It has ceased long since, sir," responded Tom, "and I would stay, if it were possible."

" Your father is anxious about you," said the doctor. " He asks where you are, and why you keep away from him. He has sent me to see what you are doing."

"I will go to him."

"You must remember your cousin is not likely to nurse him for many days, even should he live as long," remarked the doctor.

"Doctor Smiles, I am in trouble. I cannot explain, but I have much upon my mind, and I should do harm by staying," said Tom, hurriedly. "Why, my own father will be the first to urge me to depart, when I have told him everything."

"I have done my duty," said the doctor, "and when I look in this evening I shall hope to find you here."

"It is not likely," muttered the younger man.

When Doctor Smiles had departed, Tom went at once to his father's room, full of the new project which he had formed for enlisting Sir John's sympathy with his plans. Surely Sir John Dagnell would be glad to urge him on his way, when he knew that it was in Violet Hilderbrandt's interest he was going. She was his old friend's daughter, his father had confessed at last, and Sir John had risked his life already in his effort to be of service to her.

It did not strike him that his father's moods were as variable as his stages of mortal decay, and that he was more selfish than his son, but he was assured of it when he was sitting by his side, and the old man was glancing nervously at him from the folds of the dull red shawl still draped about his head.

"I must not be left alone so long as this again," he said. "I have been cruelly treated to-day, everybody has deserted me."

He was more irritable than usual, and his clenched hand struck, with considerable violence, the arm of his chair.

"Ursula is ill, and cannot come," said Tom.

"I am better without Ursula," was the reply.

"My mother——"

"She aggravates me always. She is a hateful character," he replied. "I know, Tom, she will be very glad when I am dead."

"You must have more charity and patience, sir."

"You are a fine one to talk of charity and

patience," retorted the father. "Why the devil do you preach?—it isn't in your line."

"Then there is Marcus—he——"

"A selfish brute—don't speak of him. Why do you want to thrust on me everybody I don't care for, and get away yourself?" inquired Sir John.

"It did not strike me you cared for my attendance in particular; besides——"

"You are my favourite son, Tom," coolly asserted Sir John. "I have always been very proud of you. Don't sneak away now, as if I had the plague. It's an unfilial proceeding, and upsets me."

"I would remain with pleasure, sir; I would devote my whole time to you," said Tom, "but strange events have happened which demand my presence elsewhere."

"I don't care for strange events."

"You will think I had better go," said Tom, full of his subject now, and anxious to interest his father in it also. "Violet Hilderbrandt has left Broadlands, not to escape her pursuers, but to give herself up to them in France,

where, by following her, I may be of infinite
service."

"I don't see it—besides, I knew all this before," replied Sir John. "It's stale news to
me. She had made up her mind last night to
give herself up—she told me so—although I
went out of my way to warn her to escape.
But she would not. She was very grateful to
me, she said, but she had made up her mind,
and no argument could alter her. Mercy on
me! how terribly obstinate these women are!"

"You went out of your way to warn her?"
repeated Tom, thoughtfully.

"Yes, of course, I did," said the father.
" You were watching me sharply enough too."

"It was the one good action of your life, you
said?"

"Yes," was the reply, " That's right. It *was*
a good action, surely."

"You will do another," said Tom, " and put
me on my guard by it."

Sir John shrank back from the steadfast
gaze of his son.

"You always frighten me by that look," he

said. "There is never any peace with you."

"One more question, and the last," Tom urged persistently, "Who told you last night, Violet Hilderbrandt was in danger of arrest?"

CHAPTER XVII.

NEARING THE END.

SIR JOHN DAGNELL gave an impatient twist to the red shawl about his throat, and scowled malevolently at his son. The question was not pleasant to hear or easy to answer, and there was the spirit of resistance very strong within him.

" You want to know too much," he muttered.

" It has become necessary," answered Tom, " in a house of many plots."

" You are too curious."

" Not for my own sake," Tom continued. " You might all plot your lives out against me without my caring for the motive or the result, but last night there was danger threatening the woman I love, and you knew it, and kept it back from me."

"Are you speaking of Ursula?" said the father.

"No; of Violet Hilderbrandt."

"Ah! I was not quite certain which woman it was," said the old man, somewhat spitefully. "You see there are two of them, and they have made all the mischief."

"I want your confidence," Tom replied. "I do not care to be the only one from whom the truth is concealed."

Sir John gave another tug to his shawl.

"It is all over and done with," he said, in a low tone; "it is not fair to begin again. I am not strong enough to cope with you—I—I am—very weak to-day."

He closed his eyes, and his head drooped forwards on his chest. Tom leaned over him anxiously; his father's prostration was very manifest, and he felt his own persistence could not last against it. He must give up, or bide his time; certain it was that the time was not yet for him.

"There, there, I have done," he said; "keep your secret as long as you please. I will not trouble you any more."

The withered hand of the knight stole forth to rest upon his son's, in grateful acknowledgment of the promise which had been made; but the voice was long in answering, or thanking him.

"Tom," said Sir John, at last, "you will not go away from me, then? I haven't any friend left but you."

"I will not go away—to-day," said his son, regarding him thoughtfully.

"Nor to-morrow either, please. I may be worse to-morrow," replied the father, "or I—I may be better, and able to explain everything. I should not like you to go away to-morrow."

The morrow was on his mind. It was possible, Tom thought, that there would come new events with the morrow, but he was indifferent to them. They might not affect him in any degree, but if they did he could bear them well enough and pass them by; they appertained not to the life of Violet Hilderbrandt.

"It would be better for all in this house if I were away just now," said Tom. "I am unsettled—I say and do harsh things; I have no consideration, forethought, kindness in me. I have been more than cruel to poor Ursula."

"Is she no better?" asked Sir John.

"She is too unwell to see you to-day," replied his son.

"I suppose so," said Sir John, complacently, "and for many days, Smiles tells me. That is why I want to keep you near me, Tom—only you are so dull—of—comprehension."

He closed his eyes again as if from weakness, or as if, by assuming an attitude of repose, he could ward off further questioning from a son always terribly inquisitive. But Tom was true to his promise, and no question escaped his lips, or endeavoured to escape. Tom had lived down his curiosity, "it was over and done with," as his father had asserted, and it was profitless work to trace this evil to its source, and not without its danger. It was a bitter and miserable time of inaction, rendered more unendurable by the thought that he might have

been working in Violet Hilderbrandt's cause, and
without prejudice to others to whom he could
do neither good nor harm now. If she had not
gone away to Honfleur—if his love had not
driven her away—had not strengthened her in
her terrible resolve to put a barrier for ever between them! He walked to the window and
looked out at the sea beyond the hazy landscape in the foreground. The weather was
wild and stormy still, and great masses of
clouds lay heaped up in the distant sky, sym-
bolical of the fate which Violet had chosen for
herself. What an end to her young life, and
what an end to his vain dreaming, and Ursula's,
and all with whom he had been brought in
contact in these latter days! How the shadows
submerged everything, like those huge grey
clouds over the sea, and turn where he would
there could come never again one gleam of light
to him! That was impossible. Even the wind,
soughing dismally round that unlucky house,
moaned forth its *Miserere* to him. Not only in
the valley of the shadow of death was he standing—and nearer than he dreamed—but in the

shadow of falsehood and misery and crime, and he could not see his way beyond. They were trying to deceive him at Broadlands—all of them, it might be, in their various ways—and he had grown inured to the deception, and was too callous to protest against it. The little that he knew from one did not agree with the reluctant statement of another, and he did not know whom to trust. Let things take their course, he thought; they could bring no further harm to him.

He returned to his old seat near his father, and watched him dozing there, wondering a little at Sir John's new wish to have him at his side as the friend, protector, nurse and son—and with what new phase of caprice he would wake up presently. If he would only tire of him, if he would once again evince some of the old hostility towards him, and beg him to be gone, he thought he should be grateful for the change. His father had never loved him; in all this wasted life there had been sparse signs of affection anywhere, and towards him least of all. Why, Tom thought a little rebelliously, should he sit there and sacrifice Violet Hilderbrandt's chances to an old man's selfishness?

Then the answer came, even in Sir John Dagnell's sleep.

"Don't leave me, Tom; it will not be safe to leave me."

After a while Mrs. Coombes came in, softly and cautiously, and said in a whisper from the distance,

"Is he asleep?"

Tom looked up and nodded.

"I wish we could get him to bed," she said; "but he is so dreadfully obstinate there's no doing anything with him, and," in a very low whisper, as she came close to our hero, "I don't think it's quite Christian-like to die in that chair, believing he's getting better every minute."

"The doctor—has he warned him of his critical position?"

"Once or twice, but Sir John pays no attention."

"Poor fellow," said Tom, thoughtfully; "one should have need of a good conscience to pass away in this fashion."

"Don't leave me," muttered Sir John in his sleep again; "don't run away from me, yet awhile."

"I am with you," said Tom, assuringly, as though his father had been awake. The sleeper's voice responded to him—

"That is good of you. I may want you, Tom, at any moment—don't you see?"

Tom kept his word, and remained with his father all that weary day; he neither wrote nor read, but oscillated between the fireside and the windows which looked out upon the sea. Occasionally he glanced at his watch, and muttered, to himself "She is not there yet, she has not reached Honfleur," as though there were some solace to him in his half soliloquies.

People came in and out at various times to see Sir John—Marcus and Lady Dagnell, both together at last, strange, staring, serious, and yet unsympathic figures.

Sir John did not ask them any questions, or reply to their inquiries as to his state of health that evening. He seemed to have lost all interest in them, and they went away again, after a few words exchanged with Tom concerning Ursula.

"She is better," Lady Dagnell said to Tom's inquiry; "that is, she is conscious."

"If she would like to see me——"

"Oh, no!—I'm sure she would not," was the quick answer.

The doctor was the next visitor, and Sir John recognised him, and stretched out his skinny arm towards him immediately he entered the apartment. Dr. Smiles felt his patient's pulse, looked at his tongue, asked various questions of Mrs. Coombes, nodded to our hero as if in approval of Tom's remaining at Broadlands at his especial request, and then said, in the false, cheery tone of profession—

"We must get you to bed, Sir John. It is past nine o'clock, and you must not sit up any longer."

"I shall not go to bed," the invalid answered, "I can sleep better here."

The doctor looked towards the son, and elevated his eyebrows in surprise or compassion, it was doubtful which.

"He must have his way, I suppose," he said to Tom.

"I have had it all my life," responded the knight, "and I'm not going to give up now."

"Spoken like a brave man, Sir John," Doctor Smiles remarked, with a friendly pat on the shoulder of his patient.

"A good man is better than a brave one," said Sir John, sententiously, "and I have done some good actions in my time, remember; one only as late as yesterday. Ask him?" pointing to his son.

"That is right, I believe," answered Tom.

"I can't recall the others just at present, or I'd tell you about them," Sir John added. "Where is Ursula to-night?"

"She is not well enough to attend upon you, have you forgotten that?" replied the doctor.

"No."

"You must not fret for her."

"I will not," answered Sir John. "Is she very ill?"

"She is far from well," was the guarded reply.

"She is not going to die? That is not probable, eh!" and Sir John looked up with more keenness than he had exhibited hitherto.

"No, let us hope not," replied Dr. Smiles.

"That would be very singular," said Sir John. "If she were to die now, what a difference to me!"

"To you?" asked Tom, "why to you in particular?"

"It is too late—to answer more—of your—cursed—questions," muttered the father, completely burying his head and shoulders in the shawl forthwith.

The doctor smiled at Tom, whose grim visage did not relax in sympathy, said good night and walked towards the door, where our hero followed him and arrested his exit into the corridor.

"One minute, doctor," he said, "Ursula is no worse?"

"Oh! no," replied the doctor, "she is better, and quite calm."

"I should be glad to see her."

"She is very weak—you would do wrong to attempt it."

" Very well," said Tom. " Good night."

The doctor drew the curtains aside, opened the door somewhat suddenly, and gave a little jump back into the room.

" Good gracious, Fisher," he exclaimed, in his surprise, " how you startled me !"

" I was just a-coming in to ask how the master is to-night," said the butler, in a low hoarse voice. " They say downstairs he isn't so well, but I should like to look at him for myself, if Master Tom don't mind."

The old man rubbed his hands together, and glanced towards our hero, who said :

" No, I don't mind, Robin. Come in."

The doctor departed, and Mr. Fisher shambled across the room and round the screen to the side of Sir John Dagnell, from whose face the shawl had slipped again, and whose eyes were wide open now, and staring at his visitor.

" I hope your honour's pretty well to-night?" said Robin.

" I don't know that I am, Fisher. There's a dam—dam—damnable kind of sinking here," replied the knight, as he tapped his chest with his forefinger. "How do you feel with all your weight of years? Haven't *you* got any sinkings?"

"I'm as well and strong as ever I was in my life, Sir John," croaked Mr. Fisher.

"That's a big lie, and you have no right to aggravate me with it," replied the master. "You'll die long before me, Fisher. Mark my words."

Mr. Fisher shook his head, and chuckled in defiant scorn.

"There's not twenty-four hours of good life in him," he whispered to the son; "you never see the nose pinched like that but it means mischief."

"Silence!" muttered our hero—"you know nothing about it."

Mr. Fisher turned once more to his master.

"Are there any commands to-night, Sir John?" he asked.

"No, Fisher—no," was the reply. "You have been very rude, and I have nothing more to say to you."

"If I can be of use," added the butler, "or

Master Tom is tired of you—which is very likely—here I am, at your service."

"N—no," replied Sir John, with marked hesitation in his answer, "I don't think I shall want you."

Still Mr. Fisher made no movement to depart; he stood on the rug attentively regarding Sir John Dagnell, and rubbing one hand slowly over the other, after his usual fashion. Tom remained in the background, watchful of all this, remembering also that Mr. Fisher had been in his father's company on the night of the warning to Violet Hilderbrandt, and that from him might come presently the information he required—nay, should come, if the butler were in any way possessed of it.

Mr. Fisher spoke again.

"Your son—this son, I mean—sits up with you to-night?" asked Robin.

"Yes—he will not leave me," was the answer.

"Have you told him anything?"

"No."

"I think I would, Sir John," said the old butler, earnestly.

"Some other time—in the autumn, perhaps—not now, with Ursula so near," replied Sir John, with a strong shiver.

"Ah, well! I think I would to-night."

The old man looked at Tom significantly, stooped and stirred the fire, leaned forward, touched his master's hand, and said, "Good-bye, Sir John—and a good long rest to you."

"Thank you, Fisher—thank you."

The butler, at his old shambling pace, made for the door, with Tom Dagnell following him, as he was well prepared for. They passed into the corridor together.

"What do you know of all this, Robin? What can you tell me?" said Tom, when they were without the room.

"On the night you came back I would have told you a great deal, but you would not let me," replied Fisher.

"Ay—well?"

"I must take my own time now, Master Tom," he continued, "or leave it to Sir John. You would believe him sooner than me?"

"No."

"Presently, then, when I have my full instructions from Sir John."

"But now——"

"Now you must go back to your father; he isn't fit to be left. You may find him dead already—stone dead!"

Tom Dagnell shuddered, and stepped back.

"No, no; not so awfully near as that, Robin," he exclaimed, in horror.

"I'm not so sure. I don't like the looks of him, as I've told you already," observed the butler, "and I've asked Mrs. Coombes to sit up to-night 'on spec!'"

"Fisher!"

"You'll find me somewhere about here, too, I daresay," he added, with a comprehensive sweep of his hand. "Good night to you, Master Tom; it's been a hard sort of day, hasn't it?"

"Yes, very hard!" answered Tom.

Then the door closed between them, and our hero returned to his father's side.

CHAPTER XVIII.

THE OTHER ROOM.

ROBIN FISHER'S injunctions to Mrs. Coombes to sit up that night "on spec," might have been readily dispensed with, for that duly certificated lady had not only made every arrangement to be stirring at a moment's notice, but had been warned by more than the old butler to be on her guard, for other sakes than the master of Broadlands. Lady Dagnell had her presentiments also, and they had not been discouraged by the medical attendant—this was a house with two sick persons in it whose minds were sadly ill at ease, and there had been more uncommon things happening here of late days than the messenger of death bringing to one poor mortal its mandate to be ready. They had been waiting in Broadlands for this messenger so long that why it came not was a matter of surprise to them. There would be no astonishment—possibly but little regret, when they drew the blinds down in the many windows of the great house, and nailed a gaudy hatchment on the walls.

Mrs. Coombes was on double duty that night by express request of Lady Dagnell, whose nerves were shattered, and "required perfect rest," she said, notwithstanding that she was restless also, in her way. Mrs. Coombes had Ursula Dagnell to watch as well as Sir John although her mission to the latter principally consisted in stealing to the room where he and his son sat, both very still and quiet, with the son looking round as she entered, in token of his wakefulness.

It was singular that her turn had come to nurse Miss Dagnell—that Miss Dagnell's turn to suffer had come, too, despite her gravity, her self-possession, her hardness of demeanour, which nothing had seemed to influence till then.

That something had happened at Broadlands, that Miss Hilderbrandt had departed in great haste, and Miss Dagnell had subsequently exhibited much eccentricity, Mrs. Coombes, not an unobservant woman, had perceived very clearly; but she was not particularly curious, and was more speculative as to the amount of double fees, which she, or the institution from which she was derived, might claim for extra services thus thrust upon her.

Mrs. Coombes was not quite certain, either, that the care of Ursula Dagnell would be an improvement on the especial nursing of her uncle; on the contrary, the impression deepened by degrees that this hard, three-cornered family did not take affliction with a composure that was at all becoming. Surely it ran in these Dagnells to make the most of their ailments, and to be as restive under the chastening hand as a fretful, fever-stricken child might be. It was a companion-picture to the old knight's sick-chamber, that of Ursula Dagnell; there was plagiarism in the lady's malady, or in her mode of bearing it. The fire was burning in the grate too, midsummer though it was, and seated before it, with her thoughtful gaze bent on the flames, was Ursula Dagnell, in the same dark dress which she had worn that morning. She had struggled from her bed and dressed herself, despite all remonstrance, being perverse of disposition, like her uncle, and with the same strange fancy of insisting that she was not ill, and it was other people's crotchets to imagine that she was.

"I am certainly a little weak to-day," she murmured; "nothing more. You will see how strong I shall be to-morrow.".

Mrs. Coombes proffered the same advice which she had many times in her life given to Sir John, and with the same result.

"You would feel better in your bed, Miss Dagnell."

"I shall not go to bed to-night."

It was the echo from the sick-chamber further down the corridor, and Mrs. Coombes was not surprised at it. She made the best of her position, being a woman of tact, who did not "worry" much.

"As you please, Miss Dagnell. Will you have any refreshment?"

" No."

"You must take this medicine in a few minutes, at any rate," said Mrs. Coombes, "or Dr. Smiles will scold me in the morning."

"I shall not take any more medicine," was the irritable reply. "And I don't believe in Dr. Smiles. Anyone but he would have made me strong before this—a mere swoon, as it has been. Why cannot I walk about as usual? Where has my strength gone? Is this paralysis?'

"Good gracious, Miss Dagnell, no."

"Let me try if I can walk. I have never been ill in my life before, and it is very hard at this time. God knows," she added, bitterly, "how very hard it is on me!"

"I think I would try to rest now—not walk," suggested Mrs. Coombes, but Ursula Dagnell did not care for Mrs. Coombes's suggestions; her own will was clearly shown, as well as her new weakness, when a few minutes after wards she lay back in her cushioned chair, terribly faint with the effort she had made. It was a pale, wan, struggling figure, whose breath came short and quick, and whose thin white hands—hands of which any lady might have been proud, and that had been one of the few charms of which poor Ursula had had to boast—trembled very much as they were crossed in saint-wise fashion upon the fluttering bosom of her dress.

When she was more composed, she said—

"Is Mr. Dagnell with his father still?"

Mrs. Coombes responded in the affirmative.

"Sir John has taken a new fancy to his son, to bear with his company so long," Ursula said, almost mockingly. "And the son has not much patience—has he?"

"I—I don't know, Miss Dagnell," was the reply, "he appears, at times, a little hasty."

"Go and see what they are doing, please, Mrs. Coombes," said Ursula; "I should like to know, if I am not troubling you too much!"

Mrs. Coombes had not been very long absent from Sir John's room, but she rose at Ursula's request, and went upon the errand indicated.

When she returned, she found that Miss Dagnell had changed her seat to a smaller one by the side of the fire.

"I have been trying to walk again," she said, as if in apology to Mrs. Coombes's look of protest, "but it is a hopeless task. Had I been strong, I should have followed you out, and scared you all by my appearance."

"You would have never acted so rashly," exclaimed the nurse.

"I don't know. I am very rash," she murmured, "but I have not the strength to crawl further than from that chair to this. I must have met with an accident last night when—"

Her voice died away in faint mutterings, which were impossible to follow, but the grey eyes glanced keenly at Mrs. Coombes, as if curious to note what words had reached her ears. Mrs. Coombes was also curious, and answered—

"An accident last night, did you say?"

"I had a little fall last night, in my room, I think. But that is a long time ago, now," said Ursula, more hurriedly, "and it is not worth while talking about it. Is Sir John asleep?"

"Hardly asleep, Miss Dagnell."

"Was he speaking to his son when you went in?"

"He was saying a few words."

"What were they—can you recollect them?"

"No, Miss Dagnell. I did not hear," the nurse replied.

"Why does he not sleep?" said Ursula. "Why does his son encourage him to converse, when every minute's rest is precious?"

"If Sir John has made up his mind to talk, you may be sure he will," answered Mrs. Coombes.

"Yes, yes; and kill himself with talking, too. Why, Mrs. Coombes, they may quarrel presently. These two men have never agreed in their lives, and the father is insulting and unjust," said Ursula, with excitement.

"I am sure Mr. Thomas Dagnell will not quarrel with his father," affirmed the nurse.

"Ah! you are a very wise woman," said Ursula, satirically, and regarding Mrs. Coombes with far from a loving gaze. "But you know as much of his character as this chair—or as I do, God help me."

She rose with difficulty to her feet, and clung to the mantel-piece for support.   Mrs. Coombes rose with her, and gently guided her to her first seat before the fire, and Ursula struck faintly at her helping hands.

"I did not want to sit down here," she cried, fretfully.   "I will not have you with me, if you disobey my wishes."

"I can't tell what your wishes are, Miss Dagnell," said the nurse.

"Go and see how Sir John is."

"Why—I have only just returned."

"It is an hour ago, nearly," said Ursula.

There was a few minutes' silence after this, then she said, in a calmer tone,

"What did the doctor say of Sir John's condition to-night?"

"That he was not quite so well," was the reply.

"That he was much worse, and could not live much longer, perhaps?   That there was a change in him?" cried Ursula.

"I—I—hardly think he said as much as that," stammered Mrs. Coombes, who was doubtful of the effect of any bad news upon Miss Dagnell in her present state of weakness and excitement.

"You need not be afraid of alarming or distressing me," said Ursula, coolly. "I can bear the news of my uncle's death with equanimity; I should be glad even to hear he was released from the sufferings and misery and awful injustice of this world."

"Oh! my good young lady, don't go on so, please," Mrs. Coombes implored. "You won't cool down at all. It's very wrong."

"Is he worse, then? Have they told you so?" asked Ursula.

"Yes, they have," Mrs. Coombes confessed at last.

"Have you found my glasses?" was the next question, so quick upon the other, and so irrelevant that Mrs. Coombes began to doubt the sanity of her patient.

"No, Miss Dagnell."

"It does not matter," said Ursula, "I have a second pair in my desk."

There was another pause, during which Ursula Dagnell studied the flickering of the coal fire with as much persistency as her uncle had done, and seemed by her expression to read as grim a story from it.

"Have there been any letters, or messages, or visitors to-night?" she asked.

"Not any that I am aware," responded her attendant.

"I thought there would be. It is very strange there is no news," she said, "and all goes on in the place just as usual. As if nothing had occurred—that is the horror of it!"

"But——"

"I was not speaking to you," said Ursula, sharply.

"I beg your pardon."

Miss Dagnell presently condescended, however, to address her attendant, and in the old vein.

"I should be glad to know how my uncle is," she said, "if you will go now, Mrs. Coombes."

"If you wish it—but——"

"1 am anxious about him, and that he should not talk too much to my cousin. It will make him worse," said Ursula.

"I will creep in and warn him."

"One moment," said Ursula, as Mrs. Coombes rose and walked softly towards the door. "I want you to send my cousin here. You can remain with Sir John Dagnell till he returns."

"Is it necessary? Will it not distress you very much to see him?"

"What do you mean by that?" asked Ursula, keenly. "Why should it distress me? What have they been talking about downstairs— all those wretched servants and scandal-mongers?"

"Nothing, madam, nothing, but it is so late, and you are not strong enough for fresh excitement."

"I shall not be excited," answered Ursula, "but I should be glad to see him once more, if he will come. If he will only come!"

"For a few minutes, then; and you will promise to be calm?"

" I will be very calm."

When Mrs. Coombes was at the door she said,

" Tell him I *am* very calm ; and that I only wish to say two words."

" Very well, Miss Dagnell, if you insist," replied the nurse, as she departed on her errand.

CHAPTER XIX.

REQUIESCAT IN PACE.

URSULA DAGNELL sat staid and passive, only for the time that the door remained open between her and Mrs. Coombes; as it was closed, she rose slowly, and with her hands clutching at the mantel-shelf, peered at herself in the looking-glass above it.

It was the counterfeit presentment of one very wan and woeful at which she gazed, which she seemed to inspect with a scrutinising care, as though it were a something apart from her own being, a statue in which a keen critic might be interested. There was a long-drawn sigh escaping her at last, before she passed on from her clinging position at the mantel-piece to the wall—from the wall to a davenport, a few paces distant from her. Here she sat down, unlocked the desk, and raised the lid. There were many papers in the receptacle, and her busy hands made sad havoc with the precise order in which they had been arranged. tossing and crushing them together in hot haste. When she was successful in her search, she dragged herself back to the looking-glass to put on a pair of glasses, framed in slight gold wire, and to study the effect of them before she relapsed wearily into her chair.

"I look better in my glasses, I think," she murmured. "More like the old Ursula he cared for."

She sat there very patiently; she was fully prepared for the interview with the old lover who had passed so suddenly away from her. She turned and almost smiled a welcome to him as he came in cautiously and approached her, full of grave anxiety.

"You sent for me, Ursula," he said. "You are better?"

She nodded.

"I am very glad," he continued. "To-morrow, I hope, you will be yourself again, and prepared to forgive my being so hard and uncharitable this morning, for—but there," he hastened to add, as the expression changed upon her face, "I have not come to talk of all that has happened, of all which you have told me—of anything, in fact. I am only very glad to see you so much better, Ursula."

He leaned forwards and took her hand in his, and she did not withdraw it. There was no enmity in her heart against him for the accusations he had heaped upon her at an earlier hour, for the disclosure of his love for Violet. It seemed already as if she were prepared to lose him—as if the exultation over Violet's fate had died out with the passion she had then betrayed. She was more womanly and just now; she was the cousin whom he had thought he loved, whom he could have loved in God's good time had he never met Violet Hilderbrandt on board *The Witch.*

She did not answer him in words; speech was impossible at once, for she was weaker than she had thought, and he was kinder than she had dreamed of seeing him again, but the thin fingers pressed his slightly as if in gratitude for his gentler thoughts of her.

He relinquished her hand, and stood regarding her with interest and sadness. He felt he had been hard upon this trustful nature, and could not honestly excuse all that he had done.

"You sent for me, Ursula," he said, "and, if I have not mistaken Mrs. Coombes's message, you——"

She interrupted him.

"Yes," she said, faintly, "I wished to see you very much. I am contented now."

"There were two words you desired to say, the nurse informed me?" Tom suggested. He was anxious concerning them; he had associated them in his quick, hopeful way with his release, his liberty. Great Heaven! release and liberty, and yet Violet in prison—and he had hoped for pardon in a sentence!

"Ah, yes; two words were sufficient," she said; "quite sufficient now that we are friends. They were 'Good night.'"

Tom looked surprised, perhaps disappointed, and the expression was quickly seen by Ursula, keen-eyed as she had become again.

"I will have to trouble you with many words when I am well, Tom," she murmured. "You will spare me now, I am sure?"

"I will leave you," he said.

"No; don't go yet," was the reply.

Tom took the seat which Mrs. Coombes had recently vacated, and said—

"I must not stop too long away from him."

"Is he much worse?" she asked.

"I do not see any great difference, but the doctor warns me to be prepared, and my father is more irritable than usual."

Ursula did not respond readily.

"What has he been saying?" came the slow question at length, and with her gaze averted from him.

"Very little; I do not encourage him to talk."

"No, that would be rash," responded Ursula; "he becomes very restless then. He gets feverish—like me—and there follow delusions, and mad accusations against all who have befriended him. You must not let him talk too much, Tom."

This was a long speech for a woman as weak as Ursula, and Tom noticed the effort that it was to make it.

"Neither must you talk too much, Ursula," said Tom; "I set my interdict upon it, too."

"Very well; but don't go yet awhile," she answered.

Tom remained, at her request, but the position was painful and embarrassing, and thoughts, which he would have kept down by his strong will, seemed to grow upon him—thoughts of Violet Hilderbrandt, and of the troubles awaiting her, and lying beyond that miserable, memorable day. If he could have seized this opportunity to tell the whole story to his cousin, with all its extenuating circumstances, now that she seemed gentler and kinder; if she had not sat there so weak and fragile that an angry word, a hasty confession of his want of love for her, might kill her at the outset; if she had only been well and strong enough to listen!

And this was she who had guessed all last night, and had stolen forth in the night's storm to end her despair at one blow—she who had not cared to live an hour without him, and who was suffering from her rashness, and had yet to suffer. All his fault, too—the fault of his overweening confidence in himself and his future, his desire to give back love for love at a moment's notice, and in the fulness of his gratitude. This was the bitter end of it, and not to be avoided.

The voice, speaking again, startled him with its new clearness of intonation.

"I dare not ask what your thoughts are, Tom," she said, "and it is probable I can guess them well enough. We will put off the evil hour of explanation."

Tom rose.

"I am tiring you," he said.

"Don't go," she repeated, for the third time. 'I may not see you to-morrow—we may never meet like this again."

"I am anxious about my father," said Tom. 'I do not like to be away from him."

M 2

"Very well," replied Ursula, with a sigh, "if you wish. It is your duty."

"I will return your good night now, cousin," he said, taking her thin hand again in his, and bowing over it, like a gentleman of the old school. The fingers closed warmly upon his again, and the face was raised as if to kiss him, or to receive his kiss. He hesitated for an instant, then he stooped and kissed her.

"Good night," she murmured. "I do not see why happiness should not come to us, even at the eleventh hour, Tom. Is it so utterly impossible, do you think?"

This was verging on the one forbidden topic, and in a way that struck at him, though he would not distress her by a word that night.

"To-morrow, Ursula, we will talk of this, if you are well," he said.

"Years hence, I mean, Tom," she continued, "long years hence, when you have outgrown all the romance and folly that came too late in life for you, poor boy. When we see things as they are, and know the truth, and what is just."

"To-morrow, Ursula—to-morrow."

He was terribly anxious to be gone; her earnestness scared back his old thoughts of liberty, and his heart was very heavy. She did not dream of his renunciation of her then—Violet Hilderbrandt was set apart from him for ever, she thought, and the shadow of the foreign prison lay like a bar across the path by which she might return.

"We are both young,—comparatively," she added, with another sigh, "and can afford to wait. You will remember that, Tom?—and good night again."

"Good night."

He had not reached the door when it opened, and Mrs. Coombes came in, perhaps with a little more celerity than she had hitherto shown in that establishment, but still at a grave and decorous pace enough. There was something in her looks which Tom was quick to read.

"My father?" he exclaimed.

"I think he would be glad of your company again, sir, if you are quite disengaged," she said, very calmly.

Tom departed, and Mrs. Coombes followed him into the corridor. It was for an instant only, and the nurse had re-entered, closed the door, and approached the fireside before Ursula had composed herself in her chair.

"Will you take your medicine now, Miss Dagnell?" said the nurse.

"Yes, if you please," she replied.

"Why, you are wearing your spectacles again," said Mrs. Coombes. "Come, that's well."

"Yes," answered Ursula, "that's well."

Mrs. Coombes poured out and administered a dose of Doctor Smiles's mixture, and then sat down composed and bland. Ursula twined her hands together, placed them behind her neck as if for extra support, and then "fixed" Mrs. Coombes with a steady, searching stare.

"Sir John Dagnell is worse?" she said.

"I—I never said so, ma'am," replied Mrs. Coombes, taken off her guard by this assertion.

"I have told you I can bear the shock, and it is useless to attempt to deceive me with your shallowness," said Ursula; "is he worse?"

"I am afraid he is."

"Much worse?"

"Yes."

"He should not be left to die with a nervous and excitable son," said Ursula. "I—I think I'll go to him. I am almost strong enough."

"No, no, Miss Dagnell, I hope you will not attempt it. It is no good—it is no fit scene for you," said Mrs. Coombes, imploringly. "I called Mr. Fisher, who was in the lobby, and they are all with Sir John now—Mr. Marcus and Lady Dagnell, too, I think."

"It is very sudden at the last," said Ursula, calmly; "but we have been prepared so long that it comes not like a blow. I am not surprised."

"And pray do not give way, please."

"I have borne too much to-day to give way at this," was Ursula's reply.

The two women relapsed into silence, and it was evident that the sick and ailing was the more self-possessed at this crisis of the house of Dagnell. The face was set and immobile, and the grey eyes were bright and dry in the firelight at which they gazed. Presently Ursula spoke again, and with a decisiveness that struck her listener with surprise.

"It is a base, bad life passing away," she said, "and there is no one to regret it."

"Oh! I wouldn't say it, Miss Dagnell, if I thought it," exclaimed the nurse; "and not at such a time."

"I am plain-spoken—it is my failing," answered Ursula.

"I am sure Mr. Thomas is very sorry—very much grieved indeed," said Mrs. Coombes. "Why, I am sorry myself. I have been so much with the old gentleman."

"You may be sorry—for your place," Ursula remarked, quietly. "And the younger son may be sorry, for a while, for he is forgetful and forgiving, and with a child's heart rather than a man's. And to be led like a child, and for his own good, I pray to God!"

She unclasped her hands from her neck and held them on her breast in an attitude of prayer; in her thought for the old lover she had already forgotten that the soul of Sir John

Dagnell was passing away to its judgment.

Footsteps reverberating along the corridor took Mrs. Coombes—a nurse out of her place and not in at the death, and thus doubly aggrieved—to the door, which she opened with alacrity.

Some one was passing at the moment, but Ursula Dagnell was not listening or caring.

"Is that you, Mr. Fisher?"

"Yes, ma'am, it is," responded the old butler.

"Is it—all over?"

"Yes, ma'am, it is all over. He went off nice and comfor'ble."

And this was the peaceful end of Sir John Dagnell, of Broadlands, and erewhile of the City of London, merchant.

BOOK IV.

THE LINKS OF THE CHAIN.

CHAPTER I.

UNTIMELY VISITORS.

TWO days have elapsed since the decease of Sir John Dagnell, and the house beyond Littlehampton was still in mourning for its lord and master. The white blinds were drawn down, or the shutters closed, before every window, the hatchment was already in its place, nailed like a gaudy sign-board of pride and foolish pomp to the brickwork of the building, and all that was left of the City knight reposed in its oaken case in the room where he had departed this mortal life, and was now awaiting Christian burial.

It was an ill-chosen time for visitors to Broadlands, and it was an unexpected ghastly sight to them, as they were driven through the open gates and along the carriage drive to the entrance doors.

"Why, God bless my soul, Polly, look here— look at the shutters and blinds. He's off, depend upon it!" said Mr. Oliver to his wife, sitting placidly by his side in an open vehicle hired at the station.

"Well, really—I think he is. Oh! dear, what shall we do, Jonathan?"

"I hope it is not anybody else," said Mr. Oliver, which was hardly kind to Sir John, or Sir John's remains, although not uttered with an uncharitable thought, "and that the boys are at home to talk to us a bit."

"It is a most unfortunate time to call, Jonathan."

"Yes, so it is," asserted Mr. Oliver, "although people must die at some time or other, and the hottest flares away the fastest, just like coals."

"I don't think I'd say anything in there about Sir John flaring away," mildly remarked Mrs. Oliver; "they might take it in a different light, and think you mean——"

"My dear, I don't mean anything of the sort," said Mr. Oliver. "It isn't likely."

"No, Jonathan, I thought not," replied his wife, "but you do blurt out things, sometimes, very awkward like."

"I don't profess to be polished in anything but my dish-covers," said Mr. Oliver, with a friendly nudge in Mrs. Oliver's side, and a double-knock kind of laugh at his own little joke, which gave so much play to his features that the servant opening the door caught the manufacturer with a most unseemly grin upon his broad countenance.

Mr. Oliver and his wife descended from the fly, greatly to the astonishment of the servant, who had expected cards and kind inquiries at the utmost, and at that early hour of the day.

"Is Mr. Marcus Dagnell in, or his brother?" asked Mr. Oliver.

"Yes, sir, they are in," replied the servant, "but——"

"Will you give Mr. Marcus and his brother these cards?" said Mr. Oliver, interrupting him. "We will not detain them many minutes, and

you will please say we are very sorry to find
there's a death in the house and to intrude at
such a time, of course, but that we have come
from Birmingham on purpose to see them on
important business, and should be glad of a few
minutes' interview. There, do you think you
can recollect all that?"

" Yes, sir."

"And my compliments to the rest of them—
Lady Dagnell, and Miss Dagnell, for I suppose
it's Sir John that's gone," added Mr. Oliver.

The servant ushered them into the darkened
drawing-room, where they sat down on the
couch, side by side again, as we have seen them
on the party night at Elmslie House, and waited
for the brothers' coming.

The brothers were not quick in making their
appearance, and husband and wife had leisure
to look round them, so far as the dim light
above the heavy shutters would permit.

"They've got a nice place here, Polly—plenty
of gold and blue satin about," said Mr. Oliver,
in a low tone; "it didn't strike me they were
quite as stylish as this."

"What a time they are—what a dreadfully dull place!" said his wife. "I suppose Sir John did not die of anything catching; just as we are going to see our dear girl, too."

"I suppose not. I don't think much of the pictures," Mr. Oliver muttered; "and there is not a decent bit of china in the whole room. All show, Polly, and no real value in anything. All——"

The door opened and cut short Mr. Oliver's criticism. It was Marcus who came in slowly and carefully, and with the eyeglass in his eye.

"By gad, so it is!" he said, when he had advanced very closely to them. "How are you, Mr. Oliver—how do you do, Mrs. Oliver? Beastly dark, isn't it, with these shutters closed. But we can't help that, just at present."

He shook hands with his Birmingham friends, and then sat down and faced them.

"Tom will be here in a minute. They have gone to look for him; he's walking about the garden somewhere. How's business?" asked Marcus.

"Nothing to complain of, and that is saying a great deal in these times, Marco," Mr. Oliver answered.

"Yes, exactly."

They were all three at a loss for further conversation after this. Mrs. Oliver was the first to resume it.

"So the poor old gentleman's gone, Marcus," she said.

"Thank you—yes—he's gone," was Marcus's absent reply. "Will you take anything—you have come a long way?"

"We have come by easy stages, Mrs. Oliver not being much of a traveller," said Mr. Oliver. "We were in Brighton last night. Fine place Brighton, sir!"

"Yes. Lots of fish—at the Aquarium," said Marcus. "I suppose you went there? We had Slitherwick and—his wife—about here a little while ago. They're looking very well, too."

"Ah!" said Mr. Oliver, greatly relieved at the turn which the conversation had taken, "that is what we have come about—Polly and I. For

you have been upon our minds a tremendous
deal, Marcus, since that marriage, and we
could not feel it our duty to keep away,
and not say something to you in explanation."

"I'd rather you wouldn't say anything,
please," said Marcus, regarding these honest
folk with alarm. " I don't want any long talk
over what cannot be helped ; and this is hardly
the time for it."

" And we haven't come for a long talk, either,
Marcus," said Mr. Oliver.

" That's deuced kind of you ; but—oh ! here's
Tom. I am glad they have found him, he can
talk to you like anything, and about anything ;
it's in his line," said Marcus.

Tom had entered during this speech, and
shaken hands with the Olivers, regarding them,
meanwhile, very closely, as if there might be
something to gather from their looks that might
be news of moment to him. It was a sterner,
graver face than Marcus's, full of the resolution
and strength which the elder brother's had never
expressed.

N 2

"Have you come from your daughter? Have you heard anything to-day from France?" Tom asked, quickly.

"We have come from Birmingham to see Marcus," replied Mr. Oliver; "to let him know it wasn't any fault of ours that Fanny behaved so shabbily to your brother."

"Yes, it was shabby," said Tom, somewhat impatiently; "but it is not worth apologizing for, or talking about, especially to him. What does it matter now to any of us?"

"It matters a great deal to me, Tom," Mr. Oliver replied, warmly, "or I would not have taken all this trouble to come here to say it; and I hope you're not going to choke me off this time before I can get the words out of my mouth."

"Proceed, Mr. Oliver. I will not interrupt you again," said Tom. He leaned back in his chair, folded his arms, and relapsed into a listless attitude, with his thoughts travelling very fast away, and the words falling almost meaninglessly upon his ears.

"It isn't much I have to say," the manufacturer continued, " but it's only fair I should say it, for my wife and me, once more. It wasn't any fault of ours that Fanny ran off with Mr. Slitherwick—who didn't act quite straight and proper either—although in any business transaction there is not a longer-headed fellow, or one more to be relied on. We have both felt this a good deal, and we thought we'd come and tell you as soon as ever it was possible—and my contract with the Turkish Government was finished off—and here we are to own that our daughter Fanny, on whom we have spent many thousands, has disappointed us, and made us feel smaller than ever we have done since we got out of the retail trade in the Minories."

" Don't mention it," said Marcus, after waiting for Tom's reply, as though it were more his brother's business than his own, "it is not worth taking any further notice of—upon my honour, it is not."

" That's all we have to remark—as a duty to ourselves," said Mr. Oliver, rising, "and I thought it would be better than writing to you

—for I hate writing. I'm sorry we've bother-
ed you. We would have put it off, if we had
known what had happened—but that you will
excuse. And there's no ill-will on either side,
I hope?"

"Not at all," said Marcus.

"I'm glad of that. Shake hands upon it."

Marcus put his hand in that of the manufacturer, and wished he had not when he felt
the vice-like grip of the man who was to have
been his father-in-law.

"And you, Mr. Tom?" said Mr. Oliver, when
he had done with Marcus.

Tom rose and shook hands with him, at this
appeal.

"So we forget and forgive all round, and
that's Christian-like and square," exclaimed Mr.
Oliver. "And if you don't think we connived
at getting Fanny off, we're very happy now.
Of course, we have forgiven Fanny—an only
child, full of romantic rubbish, but as good as
gold—and we're going to tell her we have been
here. If there are any commands, Marcus,
we——"

"She knows," said Marcus. "I have seen her."

"You are going to Paris," said Tom, suddenly betraying great interest again. "To-day?"

"Yes, to-day. For the first holiday in my life," answered the manufacturer.

"Have you heard that Miss Hilderbrandt surrendered herself to the French authorities two nights ago, and denied the charge which had been made against her," cried Tom. "Fanny and her husband have taken up the case, and are working earnestly for her. I have heard from them both—will you tell them how grateful I am? Will you go and study the case for yourself, with all your Birmingham shrewdness, and your money, too, which I will repay—for you must not spare money anywhere to procure the best counsel in France, and do your best in every way."

"Bless my soul, you are as impetuous as ever, and I can't follow you quite," said Mr. Oliver. "Miss Hilderbrandt a prisoner—about the diamonds, I suppose? Ah, yes, I remember when she told us both. Dear, dear, I begin to understand. Poor young girl—I liked her very much—what sentence will she get, do you think?"

"They shall acknowledge her innocence, man. Good God! What do you mean by sentence?"

"No, no—I don't mean sentence, of course—but I mean this, Mr. Tom," said Mr. Oliver, "that she will have two more friends in France this evening, who will do everything in their power for her. Everything."

"Thank you, thank you," said Tom, "they will not let you see her, but you can work in her interest for me, and until I can get away from this awful prison-house. I shall be in Paris shortly, meanwhile write to me, telegraph every hour, leave not a stone unturned for this injured girl's sake. Fancy your own daughter reduced to such a strait as this, and fighting with truth upon her side, in vain."

"Not in vain. We won't own that yet," said Mr. Oliver.

"And this Hilderbrandt—make every inquiry

concerning him. It may be valuable," ran on Tom, "I will be in Paris the day after the funeral. An hour after, I shall start from Broadlands."

The Olivers departed, and Marcus and Tom sat down again in the drawing-room.

"I wish you would think of something else besides Miss Hilderbrandt for a little while, Tom," Marcus implored, "we have a great deal to arrange."

"I am mad with suspense and inaction. It is hard that I should be the only one not moving in her cause," said Tom.

"She wished it herself," said Marcus; "besides——"

"Yes, yes, don't explain," cried Tom, interrupting him, "I know what has happened, what has to be done, and why I am tied here. How is Ursula?"

"Still very weak, the doctor says," replied Marcus; "she has been asking for you, once or twice."

"I will see her presently. Why does she not get stronger?" said Tom, fretfully. "She should be able to come downstairs, and help us all with her advice."

"Lady Dagnell says Ursula does not seem to care about our arrangements, but then——"

"But then Lady Dagnell is very busy with her mourning," concluded Tom, bitterly, "and requires a deal of interest to be shown in it by us all. Do you think I am really of any service, Marcus?"

"I don't know what we should do without you," Marcus confessed, "I'm a regular fool myself, just at present."

"I will give you one fair warning," said Tom, decisively, "that I remain in this house conditionally, and that any new turn of events, at Paris or here, which affects Violet Hilderbrandt, and points to either hope or danger, and I leave at once."

"What, before——"

"Before everything is the living," said Tom, sternly, "the dead can afford to wait."

"Ah! yes, exactly," replied Marcus, "but you need not tell us just now. I should like to get out of the house myself, awfully, but——Hallo,

Fisher, what is it you want, bobbing in like that?"

"It's some one for Master Tom," said Fisher, in a husky whisper, "and a rum one he is too. He won't go away for anybody, until he's seen you."

"What is his name?"

"Times, or Slimes," replied the butler, "Larry Slimes. He was here two days ago, he says, but I didn't catch sight of the vagabone myself."

"He must come this way at once. Quick, Fisher, show him in! Marcus," said Tom, turning to his brother, "this is the bearer of news, good or bad, and of life value to me. The dead will have to wait now!"

CHAPTER II.

REVELATION.

THE waif and scarecrow who has vaguely flitted through these pages like a bird of evil omen, for ever presaging disaster, as Tom had designated him on one occasion, was to be true to his character to the last. Our hero had looked forward to news of Violet Hilderbrandt, this child of the streets having always brought him tidings of her, but on this occasion he was doomed to disappointment.

Mr. Fisher ushered in Larry Simes with a contemptuous " Here he is, then !" and Larry, in his usual sidelong fashion when out of his element, and with the " proprieties " dismaying him, slouched into the room, twisting his cap in his hands, and craning his neck forwards to make sure of the identity of those who were waiting for him in the shadows.

"Well, Larry," said Tom. "what news of Miss Hilderbrandt?—quick."

"I don't know nuffink of her," answered Larry, sullenly. "I ain't heard nuffink—I don't want to."

"What has brought you here?" Tom inquired.

"I'll be round to that in a minit, if yer'll give a cove time to get a breath," he said. "May I sit down, guv'nor, on this?"

"Yes, sit down," Tom replied.

"Thankee. I'm floored with my walk—blest if I ain't. And such a ketchin' here, guv'nor" —laying his hand and cap upon his narrow chest,—"as if sumfink was a-grabbin' me inside —orful."

Larry Simes sank into one of the blue satin easy-chairs, where he looked woefully out of place, and where it was as well that the light of day shone not very clearly on him.

"Are you ill?" asked Tom.

"I feels jest as if I'm in for a fever agin. I'm ollers havin' fevers, cussed if I ain't!" said the aggrieved Larry.

"Gracious gad!" exclaimed Marcus, "hadn't he better go, Tom?"

"Let him be," said Tom; "he has not come all this way for nothing."

"N—no—exactly; but you'll excuse me, I hope," said Marcus. "I shouldn't like to catch anything myself just now."

The elder brother beat a hasty retreat, returning to look round the door for a fleeting moment again.

"I think I would clear him off the premises, Tom, as soon as convenient," he suggested; then he closed the door and retired.

"That's your brother, ain't it?" asked Larry.

"Yes—my brother."

"A starchy bloke, ain't he!" Larry added. "I shouldn't like to ax a favor of *him*."

"Do you want a favour of me, then?" asked Tom.

"Yer gave me a quid when I last spotted yer," said Larry. "Yer isn't a bad sort of a swell, and I likes yer. I don't know as how I ever had a civil word from any cove afore, but I'd do anythink for yer I could, and that's gord's truth."

"I'm afraid you can do nothing for me, Larry," answered Tom.

"Not in Bumminghum?" added Larry.

"No," said Tom; "and now what can I do for you? Help you on your way? I suppose you want help in that direction?"

"That's jist it."

"I don't see what claim you have upon me, boy, save that you brought me once a warning to a friend," said Tom, "but if you are hard up, I shall not say No."

"Thankee."

Larry sat and thought deeply after this, and it was not till Tom said, somewhat sharply, "Well, what is it?" that he appeared to rouse himself.

"I wants to borrer my fare 'ome, and if yer'll make it ten bob over, I shan't forget it in a nurry. That ain't," he added, wistfully, "puttin' the big pot on too much?"

"You shall have the money."

"Thankee," he said again. "Dessay yer wonders now where I've melted the last quid, but I stood drinks to a lot o' coves, and they prigged the rest on it while I was asleep. I'm cleaned out, or I would not have come round agin," added Larry, in half apology, "for I hates cadgin'."

"What will you do in Birmingham?"

"The same old game, guv'nor, I thinks," answered Larry; "there's nuffink else I've been dragged up to, or is fit for. I shall be out o' the fever in a week or two—if it is fever, for I ain't so certin. Only these gallersed shakes seem like it."

"There's money for you," said Tom, "and now be off, and never let me see you again, without you're honest."

"All right. Thankee—yer werry good."

Larry took the money proffered him, spat on it, with his usual ceremony, put it in his trousers' pocket, and rose slowly and painfully.

"I went and looked at that sea agin," he remarked, suddenly, "but it wouldn't wash."

"What do you mean?" said Tom.

"Didn't yer tell me to go to sea? Well, I couldn't go muckin' about in a collier—it ain't my line—and I feels the cold too orful bad," Larry explained, "but I thought, arter wot you said, I'd have a try. No use—nuffink's no use!" he added, almost sadly.

"Try again, Larry."

"Shan't," was his quick retort, turning and snapping as a dog might have done at a friendly hand—"I tell yer I shan't ever agin!"

"Good morning," said Tom, quietly.

Larry seemed a little bit ashamed of his petulant outburst. He stood twisting his cap in his hands, and regarding our hero furtively.

"And there's nuffink I can do for yer?" he muttered.

A sudden thought came to Tom as the boy spoke.

"Yes, there is."

"Wot is it?" asked Larry, with alacrity.

"Tell me where I can find this Hilderbrandt. You must know—he has written to you. You have telegraphed to him."

Larry hesitated.

"He ain't been fair with me——" he said, "he's left me anyhow, and I ain't afeard o' him. I can live on my own hook, well enuf. Yer won't split on him, I spose?" he added, doubt-fully.

"No," said Tom.

"He's in London, then. Do yer know London?"

"Yes."

"Do yer know the Strand?" was the next inquiry.

"Yes,"

"Do yer know number 'leven 'undred and nine!" continued Larry.

"I can discover it," Tom replied.

"Wery well, ax for Mr. Harnett," said Larry, "and yer'll find him, unless he's a stiff un by this time, as I wish I wos."

Tom hastily entered the address down in his pocket-book, and then turned to the morbid Larry again.

"When I looked at all that water I wos a-tellin' yer about," said Larry, as he moved towards the door, "I wished I'd had the pluck o' that sarvant gal o' yourn, who tried to drown herself the night afore I saw yer, but I ain't up to it, guv'nor."

"Ha! what do you know of that?" said Tom, surprised.

"I wos a-watchin' her, to be sure," was the answer. "I helped to get her out. I can't swim, but I ran in arter her, an' the dog follered, and 'ead over 'eels, 'eels over 'ead, went the three on us, over and over, and wops we come aginst the breakwater two or three times afore we bashed upon the sands again. I couldn't see the gal drown, and in I went, and that's how I've caught these blooming creeps."

"You saved my cousin's life, Larry," exclaimed Tom, "and thank you."

"Yer cussin!" echoed Larry, with his lower jaw dropping.

"Yes, my cousin."

"Wot, that gal?" cried Larry, in disgust, "wot, that liar? Oh! s'elp me."

"Liar?" cried Tom; "why liar?"

"She said she wos a sarvant gal, lady's or

sumfink maid up at the 'ouse. I'd been follerin' her for a skit of a time all over the town, direckly she come out fust, and went off to the staishun-'ouse, yer know?"

"WHAT!" shouted Tom, so vehemently that Larry ran against the door in sudden alarm, and cowered from his questioner.

"The staishun-'ouse. I said so."

"God of heaven!" ejaculated Tom Dagnell.

"She put the Peelers on to yer gal. Didn't yer twig? Didn't yer——"

"Are you sure of this?" cried Tom. "Are you really sure, boy? Try to think again?"

"Oh! it's right enuf—here's the specs' she dropped a-coming out. She took 'em off to write. I saw her over the winder blind."

"And then?"

"And then she went off at a trot bang over the fields, and slap into the sea?"

"You may go, Larry." said Tom, in a hollow voice, as Larry put the spectacles into his hands; "I don't care to hear any more."

"All right," answered Larry, "I didn't mean to say anythink o' this; she axed me not, and

we've got the gal away all right. But to think
she's your cussin—rum, ain't it?"

"Go now, will you?" Tom said again.

They were the last words he ever heard from
Larry Simes. The stormy petrel spread his
dusky wings and took his flight for ever from
Tom Dagnell. He had brought with him a new
element of horror, and it remained at Broadlands after he had passed upon his way. It held
the man who had received it in bondage and in
stupor, as though he had been struck by a giant's
hand. He sat there in the house of mourning,
in a great darkness of mind, a stern silent figure
on whom no light was falling, and to whom it
seemed no light could come again.

CHAPTER III.

AFTER THE VISIT.

IT was Lady Dagnell who found her younger son sitting in the drawing-room. An hour had passed since Larry Simes had departed, and Tom had not moved from his position.

"Mercy on me, Thomas," exclaimed Lady Dagnell. "Is it absolutely necessary for you to sit in this dreadfully dark room?"

"It has been, mother," he replied. "I have had much to think out."

"And you will excuse me, but I do not really see why you should grieve in this outrageous manner for your poor father," she added. "There are limits to earthly sorrow. I don't give way myself too much, and yet I am far from strong at the best of times."

"I am not grieving for my father," answered the son.

"Indeed!"

"I have had a greater loss than his."

"Is anyone else dead?" inquired Lady Dagnell. "Break it gently to me, if there is."

"I have lost all faith—all——"

He stopped suddenly. His mother was not a woman to take into his confidence. There was no one at Broadlands in whom he could confide; no one, perhaps, in all the world to whom he could tell the story.

"Where's Ursula?" he asked.

"Ursula, did you say? She is in her room, of course; she is always in her room now. Do you want to see her?"

"Not at present," he added, after a moment's further consideration of the matter.

"Upon my word, my son, I do not comprehend you clearly to-day," said Lady Dagnell.

"It's no use trying, mother; I am not certain if I am awake from a bad dream," Tom answered.

Lady Dagnell grew somewhat nervous of her

son. Anything out of the common way had been always calculated to alarm her—she had lived all her life in an atmosphere of little scares.

"You have been sitting in the dark too long," said Lady Dagnell; "why don't you go for a long walk in the park, or for a ride to Arundel, or—no, I should not care to be left in the house without you, now I come to think of it."

"You got on very well without me for years," said Tom, a little bitterly, perhaps.

"Ah! I mean at this time—this solemn occasion, Thomas," replied his mother.

"When is the funeral?" asked Tom.

"Why, you know!" exclaimed Lady Dagnell; "you have made all the arrangements yourself, except a few alterations of my own, which I think calculated to give dignity to the painful ceremony."

"Alteration!" said Tom. "Ah, well, when is the funeral, do you say?"

"You are aware as well as I am that it is four days hence," replied Lady Dagnell; "how can you go on like this, unless you wish to frighten me?"

"I had forgotten," replied Tom, "and I am hardly awake, I tell you. In four days, then, I shall be back at Broadlands; you may rely upon my coming."

"My dear son, you will not leave us?"

"Yes, I must go."

"At such a distressing time, with Ursula so poorly, and poor, dear, dead Sir John in the house awaiting Christian burial; I cannot believe it."

"Mother," said Tom, "I have important business which I dare not neglect."

"You are going to France!" cried Lady Dagnell. "Oh! I am sure you are."

"I am going to London."

"Well, well, Thomas, I must say it is not paying a proper respect to the deceased," said his mother.

"I told Marcus I should think of the living before the dead," answered Tom.

"It's absolutely indecent and cruel," said Lady Dagnell, whimpering. "I'm one of the living, and you are doing your best to throw me on a sick-bed. What business can take you to town?"

Tom did not answer until his mother repeated the question, when he said,

"I can trust no one in this house—don't ask me."

Lady Dagnell withdrew after this affront, but not without a Parthian dart at him.

"If Sir John had been alive, you would not have insulted me in this manner," she said. "I —I have lost my only friend and comforter now, and you turn upon me like the thankless child that you are."

She waited at the door for her son to succumb, to express his regret, and to promise to remain at Broadlands, but not a word escaped him, and she closed the door behind her at last with a formidable slam. Half an hour afterwards she was in Ursula Dagnell's room— although her feelings had not altered in any way towards Ursula, whom she persistently disliked. She could disguise her antipathies at times with a fair amount of womanly skill, and in this instance she entered, full of a rare sympathy and anxiety.

"My dear Ursula, 1 hope you're better to-

day," she said. " I have dreadful news for you,
and I want your co-operation. If you can't
stop what is going on, no one else can, and we
must not be left here with only the servants and
Marcus. And Marcus is not the least bit of good,
is he ?"

Ursula had not grown stronger in any great
degree since the night on which her uncle died,
but she stood up, very straight and rigid, as
Lady Dagnell completed her extraordinary appeal.

" What have you to say ?" she asked, almost
contemptuously. " Will it please your ladyship
to be coherent ?"

Lady Dagnell had been already coherent
enough for her niece, but she went on :

" Tom is going to leave us."

" Now ?" said Ursula, in a different tone.

" At once. He says he has business in town.
As if that were likely, at this sad time," she
cried.

" Did he tell you what business ?"

" Not a word," replied Lady Dagnell. " He
flew into a passion, and said he could not trust

anybody in this house. He has shattered my nerves completely. I don't know what I shall do for the rest of the day. I am unhinged."

"You will require a stimulant," said Ursula.

Lady Dagnell glanced askance at her niece, as if suspecting a cruel irony in the remark, but Ursula's face betrayed only a deep study of matters more serious than the condition of her aunt's nerves.

"Has he had any fresh news from France?" asked Ursula.

"Not since the morning."

"Has anyone called?"

"I don't know. I have not asked," replied the aunt.

Ursula touched the bell, and Mrs. Coombes, still on duty at Broadlands, and now in Miss Dagnell's service, entered at the summons.

"Will you be good enough to find out for me, Mrs. Coombes, what visitors have called to-day, and who has seen them?" said Ursula.

"Yes, Miss Dagnell."

Ursula sat down with her hand pressed suddenly to her side.

"What is the matter?" exclaimed Lady Dagnell. "How you have startled me! What dreadful faces you are making! Shall I——"

"A passing spasm to which I have got used," said Ursula. "I had hoped to be free from pain to-day. I got up this morning with almost a light heart."

"Ah! a little thing upsets you—as it does me, Ursula," was Lady Dagnell's comment.

"I don't think so," said Ursula.

Lady Dagnell disliked contradiction, and frowned a little at the last remark. She would probably have expressed an opinion concerning it, had not Mrs. Coombes re-entered, and imparted the news that Mr. and Mrs. Oliver had called with kind condolences, and seen both Tom and Marcus in the drawing-room—and that afterwards a ragged lad, who said his name was Simes, had been in consultation with Mr. Thomas Dagnell.

Ursula closed her eyes, as if she could listen with more composure thus, but the two women watching her noticed how the old greyness, as of a death in life, settled upon the face again, and remained there.

When Mrs. Coombes was leaning over her the eyes opened, and Ursula said, petulantly,

"I am not ill. I am not partial to fainting-fits, like that Violet Hilderbrandt. There has been nothing to excite me. Why do you keep staring at me—you two women?"

"I was afraid you were not well," Mrs. Coombes replied.

"I am quite well—I am going downstairs for the first time to-day," said Ursula, " although I am fond of this room, and all its peace and quietness—its happy memory of his coming with kind words to me. Think of it soon—to *me!*"

She rose and walked steadily across the room towards the door.

"Are you going downstairs?" asked Lady Dagnell.

"Yes."

"To use your influence with my son to induce him to remain, I hope," said Lady Dagnell. "He will listen to you when he will not heed anybody else."

"Ah! but then how fond he is of me!" was the hollow response.

"You will put this shawl over your shoulders, before you go down for the first time," said Mrs. Coombes, spreading out the article in question, and making a movement to wrap it round her new patient.

"Take it away," cried Ursula, sharply. "I don't want it."

She passed into the corridor, and walked slowly its length to the grand staircase, in the middle of which she came to a full stop, and thought so long and deeply that the servants in the hall caught sight of her, and wondered why she paused. She came slowly on once more to the great skin mat upon the chequered marble of the entrance-hall.

"Where is your master?" she asked of one of the footmen who had been looking up at her.

"Mr. Marcus is——"

"I said your master," said Ursula; "Mr. Tom Dagnell will be your master here. Don't forget that, if you care to keep your place."

"Mr. Thomas is in the park, ma'am," replied

the servant. "I saw him go out a little while ago."

"Has he gone—for good?" she almost hissed at him.

"No, madam," said the servant, backing a step or two. "He hasn't got his hat on."

"I—I thought he could not have left," said Ursula, in a different and calmer tone, "but you surprised me."

"Shall I tell him you wish to see him, Miss Dagnell?" asked the servant, "he's——"

"No. I will find him for myself."

And then, bareheaded, and walking very slowly still, but with an erect and stately mien, Ursula Dagnell passed from the house of death into the free air and sunshine beyond it.

CHAPTER IV.

THE OLD SERVANT.

A MAN not prone to take advice at the best of times, and who by rejecting it occasionally had made many grave mistakes, Tom Dagnell had in this instance followed his mother's instructions to seek the park-land beyond the house in preference to the gloom of the drawing-room, where Lady Dagnell had discovered him.

There was more space for thought in the great park; he could not leave for London yet awhile, he had discovered by the time-table, and here he could wander on undisturbed, he hoped, and endeavour to fashion into shape the future course of his life. Everything had changed since the morning, even his own estimate of the poor humanity about him.

He was right; there was no trusting anyone at Broadlands, and he must think for himself, now that there was so much deceit in his way.

He would have consideration for no one but Violet Hilderbrandt; it was his right, he thought, born of the treachery which had been at work against her from the first, born of the love too which had grown with him, and which he knew was as hopeless as Ursula's hate of her had made it.

He went far into the woodland; and at so swift a pace that Ursula would have sought him in vain, had he not turned to retrace his steps at the same fierce rate of progression, and was once more, and unconsciously, approaching her from whose presence he would have prayed God to spare him had he known how close she was upon him then.

The crisis of this last meeting was not to come at once, for Fate, in the shape of Robin Fisher—and there could not have been a grimmer, harder fate in that hour—was to balk the one faint chance which Ursula Dagnell might have had. It was the old butler wandering about the park also, perhaps putting himself intentionally in the young master's way, upon whom Tom Dagnell chanced before he was aware.

At the first glimpse of him, Tom turned with the intention of walking hastily away, then a new impulse made him swerve, and he came with quick long strides to the side of the old man.

" What are you doing here ?" asked Tom.

" Taking a bit of a walk—I'm going into the town about my black, through the wicket yonder," replied the butler.

" I am glad I have met you," said Tom, hurriedly, " I have heard bad news—awful news—to-day."

" This is a fine place for bad news," answered Mr. Fisher. " I don't know that I ever heard of any good in all my long time of service. I——"

" That will do. Listen to me."

" Yes, Mr. Tom."

The old man crossed his large-veined hands together, clasped them across the lower buttons of his waistcoat, and looked at Tom with half shut, blinking eyes—the sun falling strongly on his wrinkled countenance.

"If there is anyone I can trust, it is you, Robin, after all," said Tom.

"Yes, Master Tom," was the reply. "You may trust me in your interests, always. I haven't forgotten it—I have been watching, when it looked as if you had turned your back upon it—but I thought the funeral might pass over first."

"You have something to say, then?"

"Yes, I have."

"What Sir John Dagnell did not care to tell me?"

"Ay, that's it."

"What he was afraid to tell me, whilst my cousin Ursula was nursing him night after night? Is that the awful truth of it?" asked Tom.

"Ay, sir, he were maun afraid of her to the last. But"—and here the thin lips were puckered closely—"I thought I was never to say a word again' the lady any more?"

"I have learned to doubt her—I see much misery in this house, of which she has been the cause," said Tom, sternly.

"I could have given you warning of a lot of it, if you had only let me speak, but you wouldn't," muttered Mr. Fisher, thinking of his old grievance.

"Tell me all now. I must be upon my guard."

"And you ain't going to marry Miss Ursula?"

"I am not."

"We had better turn back a little way," said the butler. "You see we are in sight of the house, when we come round that bend."

The two turned, and Ursula Dagnell saw them for the first time, as they passed on side by side under the distant trees. They were walking away from her, and her strength was spent and gone. She could not overtake them; it was beyond her power. She sat down on one of the rustic benches in the park,

and waited with a seeming patience for her
cousin.   He must return that way in good
time; he must pass her there, unless he went
out into the green lanes and home by the high-
road, which was unlikely.   Bare-headed, like
the old lover, she sat under the broad-leaved
shelter of an oak-tree, and in the warm summer
air, into which she had not ventured since her
illness.   The deer came to her, and looked
curiously at her; the birds sang above her
head, and darted by her with light-glancing
wings; all was peace, and a fair harmony of
nature on that bright summer's day.

How long she waited for him, she never knew.
She had no consciousness of time—it seemed
not to belong to her life any more.   A statue
hewn of marble and set up there could have
been scarcely more inanimate than she, until
Robin Fisher, turned from his thoughts of trying on his new black suit, came with his hands
behind him, at a feeble trot, along the close
green turf.

Ursula had risen, and was standing in his
way before he was aware of it.   He glared at

her as at a ghost, which he had believed could only haunt the house itself.

"Where is my cousin, Fisher? Where have you left him?" she cried.

"Master Tom—you mean—of course?" he stammered in reply.

"Yes—where is he?" was the eager question again.

"I wouldn't go to him now, Miss Dagnell," said the butler. "He's had quite enough to bear to-day."

"I know that. So have I."

"And——"

"Where is he?" Ursula demanded for the third time.

"A little way along there," said Mr. Fisher, pointing in the direction he had come, "you can't miss him. He is walking straight towards you. Isn't that him—just by the clump of trees?"

"Yes. Now go!"

"Certainly, ma'am."

The old man recommenced his trot towards the mansion, and Ursula Dagnell moved towards her old lover for an instant. He saw her advancing, stopped, hesitated, and then came on again.

CHAPTER V.

THE LAST MEETING IN THEIR LIVES.

THIS was the end of the love-dream begun so short a while ago, and in this miserable fashion were dashed down all the hopes which delusion had fostered, and vanity and selfishness had betrayed. It was all over. Man and woman who had plighted their troth in the cold March month were to set it aside ere the June days were ended. The fates had not allowed them one clear quarter of a year to find out their mistakes—the fallacy of all that they had planned and striven for. The sands upon which their trust was built had shifted with the first great tide which had rolled towards them, changing and submerging everything.

Ursula Dagnell knew it was too late when her cousin was close upon her, and his steely looks were those of her judge and her accuser. Her last faint hope went by. This was the very end, indeed!

If she could have turned back without hearing a single word, and stolen away into some hiding-place to die, she would have been glad —it would have saved her one more bitter memory in a life that had been full of harsh reminiscence. For this was a man who would never forgive her, she could see it in his eyes already. After all, he was a Dagnell, and would have no mercy. He did not appear surprised to meet her, bare-headed, in the park—he had outlived all surprises, he thought, and there was nothing to excite or astonish him in life now. He looked with a cold, almost contemptuous, calmness at her, as a strong man might upon a foe unworthy of his steel, and who is unable by sheer weakness to hold his own against him.

Ursula thought he would walk by her, with a slight bow of recognition, but this was her mistake.

"Don't go, Tom—you must speak to me!" she said, imploringly.

"I was not going to pass you," Tom replied.

"Sit down with me, will you?" she said, indicating the rustic bench which she had quitted.

"Anywhere you please," was his answer.

They walked back to the seat she had left, and sat down side by side. She raised her eyes slowly, but the steady gaze in his it was impossible to stand against—it told so much of the truth—it regarded her as a something low, abject, and mysterious, whose motives he hardly cared to analyse, though they had been the shipwreck of his life.

"I have seen your mother, Tom," she began, in a low, quavering voice, "and she tells me you are going away to-day. Is that true?"

"Quite true, Miss Dagnell."

She shivered at the appellation he had bestowed upon her—it was so awfully strange! It was the first time in his life he had called her by that name.

"May I ask upon what errand you go, and if this is the beginning of another mystery?" she

said, more in her old tone of voice, as though
the courage to confront him were returning in
the hour of her despair.

"I have got clear of the mystery," said Tom,
"and am in the daylight, at last. I am going
to see Violet's father."

"What can he do?"

"I don't know," answered Tom Dagnell,
"but he is her father, and I wish to see him."

"It is the old mad impulse," said Ursula.

"It is the old thought for Violet Hilderbrandt,
I own it, and I am not likely to escape from it
again," cried Tom.

"And you tell *me* this?" said Ursula, drawing
herself up, rigid and firm.

"Why should I not?" was the measured answer. "What are you to me, Miss Dagnell,
now?"

"I am engaged to be married to you," was
the response.

Again the curious, contemptuous look in his
eyes—the consciousness that he was looking
down upon her as from a cliff's verge into a
deep, dark gulf wherein she might be hiding.

"And I love another woman," he said.

"Who is in prison!"

"Yes," said Tom, "and who preferred to go of her own free will, rather than it should be said in Broadlands that you tried to put her there. It is the old charge, but I make it in no heat of passion now, and with no wish to strike you down afresh."

"No, it looks like it," murmured Ursula. "I see how charitable you are."

"It is my painful task to tell you that I know this for the truth," he added—"before, I only suspected it."

"You have great faith in the statements of your spies," answered Ursula. "A servant and a thief are the witnesses against me."

"Ah! do not attempt to fight so poor a battle," said Tom; "rather confess your sins, and ask Heaven to pardon you."

"And you—what will you do?"

"I cannot forgive you," was the stern reply.

"I have nothing to repent," she said, looking

down and wringing her hands together—" nothing whatever."

" I cannot forgive you, I would have added, unless you are repentant of all the misery you have caused, but you forestall me."

" I have nothing to regret," she repeated.

Ursula Dagnell stood her ground still against the unknown facts which this man knew, and held studiously from her out of charity.

" In the drawing-room, a few days since, you called me a dastard for suspecting you," Tom continued, " and I was ready to believe you once again, but it is not possible a second time to cheat me."

Perhaps she had deemed it possible—had prayed even for the impossible—in this, and in her wild, strong love for the man sitting by her side. It was difficult to guess her thoughts, or why she fought so hard against his thoughts of her.

" I say I have nothing to repent—nothing to regret," she said again. " What is your charge against me ?"

" You gave evidence to the police that Violet Hilderbrandt was with us."

" Who says so ?"

" You told my father you should betray her; you stole away to the police-station for that purpose. Robin Fisher learned this from Sir John, who, dying as he was, went to Violet's room to urge her to escape. The infamy was beyond my father's calculation."

This was news to Ursula Dagnell, and was received strangely.

" The warning came from him then," she muttered, " and he was treacherous to the last. What good reason I have had to hate him all my life—to hate him in his coffin !"

" You own to this ?" said Tom.

" I have not said so."

Strange clinging to the falsities slipping away from her, and yet only the desperate tenacity of a false woman at bay.

" There are your glasses, left behind you at the station when you turned Queen's evidence," he said, putting the spectacles in her lap.

She brushed them from her to the grass, and set her foot upon them passionately.

"I lost them in the sea, when I went down to die," she said.

"No; it is not true."

"To die for you, Tom," she added—"to spare myself such a day as this has been, and which I knew must come. There was no concealment that could last; they took down my name and address at the police-station. It is all true, there!"

Tom rose from her side. The confession had been made, and he had no further reproaches to heap upon her. He was strong, and she was weak, and he would be glad to get away, and spare her further shame.

"But you must not leave me like this," she said, catching at his sleeve and almost dragging him down to her side once more. "I have a right to speak, and you need not fear I shall give way like a child again."

She had read his thoughts very quickly, forestalling the excuse which he would have made to leave her.

"I can bear anything after this," she added.

"What is there to say which can do any good?" said Tom, restlessly.

"Ah! that is like a man," she answered, bitterly; "the accusations and the insults have been proffered, but the defence he does not care to hear. He has made up his mind he is completely in the right."

"There is no defence worthy of the name," said Tom; "why attempt it? Say you are sorry only, and let me go away with a better opinion of you."

"I am *not* sorry," she cried. "I do not repent that woman is set apart from you. Have I nothing to complain of, do you think, or is all the deceit on my side? It was you who belonged to me, and would have been my husband but for her—it was she who lured you from me, and made my life the blight it is. Good God! Tom Dagnell, what are that woman's wrongs to mine?"

"I have been weak," Tom answered, "but I will not excuse that weakness, or ask your pardon now. I am only glad that my true knowledge of you has come before it is too late."

"I have been cruelly wronged," she said, "and you have not the manliness to own how much misery you have caused me!"

"I do not care to discuss this further," said Tom, "to ask for explanations from you of much that has happened here. I know all, and there will be time to speak presently."

"All," she repeated, "have you told me all?"

"No."

"Have you not been able to see, then, that all has been for love of you?—and that guilty as I may have been," she said, with her voice wavering at last, "I have thought only of you, as Heaven is my judge."

"No, no."

"The evil which began in this house, years ago, was not of my beginning," said Ursula.

"I know it," answered Tom, "and am sorry for my father's share."

"He was trustee to the estate *my* father left me. I was an orphan, and he robbed me of everything I had."

"On the night of my return, he told me that

awful story, and how you had forgiven him, for my sake," said Tom, sternly now, "but that was not the truth. You had not forgiven him —there was no mercy in you—for ever hanging over his head was the threat of his disgrace."

"I bore him no malice," Ursula replied; "he had robbed me at the instigation of that wretch Hilderbrandt—*her* father. The crime lay far enough back when I discovered it. I held him in my power, true, but it was for your sake. Not for mine."

"You drove a bargain with him, and I was the price. This was your mercy," said Tom. "Whatever happened, I was not to escape."

"I loved you, Tom," she murmured once more. It was her one plea—her one mad excuse for all that she had done.

"If I had only known of this unholy compact!" he cried.

"You would have hated me, as you do now," said Ursula.

"I do not hate you; I pity you."

"It is the same to me," she whispered, faintly.

"You trained my father to repeat the story

of your goodness and self-sacrifice, but in such a calculating affection I cannot believe. You deceived yourself, as well as me, when you called that love."

"Did your father tell you all, in the hour before he died?" she asked. "Oh, no! or you would not have come to me with kind words upon your lips. You would have crushed me down without remorse, as you are doing now."

"I did not wish to speak of this," said Tom; "but you have forced the whole truth from me."

"Hardly the whole truth; but I have no defence to urge," she answered, very mournfully. "I have not the heart for it. Your father's version of the story may stand. I don't care to say another word."

"When I return you will be mistress here—that fact escaped you in your passion, if you will try to recollect," said Tom.

"Your father has left me his property, every penny that he has, in atonement for all that he had robbed me of," Ursula replied. "The balance is still against me, for Sir John was unlucky, and died comparatively poor. That is my misfortune, but I cannot ask for your sympathy."

Ursula Dagnell was variable in her moods, and very womanly in consequence. This was the cold, calculating, bitter Ursula, and he was glad to see her thus; it rendered his parting with her more easy, and more natural.

"I will congratulate you instead on your prosperity," said Tom. He got up as he spoke, and she made no effort to delay him further; each seemed defiant of the other at the last. How long ago was it since Tom Dagnell had assured her that he would be true to her for ever? And how far a distance was this from his hate, let him call it "pity" if he would?

He went slowly from her towards the house, and after a while she turned and watched him, resting her hands upon the rail of the bench, and gazing after him as at the last hope in life passing away from her. Something told him she was looking after him still, warned him perhaps that he might have left her with a kinder word, a gentler look, immeasurably as she had wronged him. He had been to blame himself, he had talked of love to her, not knowing what love was—after all, what a life hers had been despite her scheming, and the present hour of triumph in her complete success. He could believe in her misery, if in nothing else. He turned back suddenly, and walked quickly to her side.

"Ursula," he said, "this is not a time to bear malice in our hearts, and I am going from you. I forgive you—good-bye."

She had expected harsher words—possibly another cruel sentence that should tell more completely how he despised her, and should burn into her heart like fire for ever afterwards —and she turned her head completely away from him and bowed it very low. She even accepted his forgiveness gratefully.

"Thank you," she murmured, hastily, and in a voice he did not know.

"Will you tell me in return, Ursula, that you are sorry for all you have done to poor Violet?"

The answer came in the same deep, stifled tones, "I am not sorry for that."

"Not sorry?"

" No !"

" When I come back to my father's funeral,
and see you again—when you and I are standing at his grave,—you will give me a fairer
answer," he said.

" This may be the last meeting in our lives,"
was Ursula's reply.

" Ursula, I pray that no fresh rashness——"

" You need not be afraid of me again," she
said, interrupting him, " you have left me in
God's hands now !"

" Good-bye."

" Good-bye."

Thus they parted, and once more Ursula
Dagnell turned her eyes towards him and
watched him walk away under the great green
trees and across the fair park land, into the
sunshine that was there. Long after he had
vanished from her for ever, she sat in the same
cold, impassive attitude, watchful—and waiting !

CHAPTER VI.

MR. HARNETT'S EMPORIUM.

THUS Tom Dagnell was fairly "off with the old love." The story was at end, the tie which had bound them so strangely together had been as strangely dissevered, and he was a free man. And yet she had not given him up by a word; she had accepted his reproaches, acknowledged how she had planned and plotted for him, and revenged herself upon the rival who had confronted her. She had thanked him for his forgiveness, expressed defiantly enough her satisfaction at Violet Hilderbrandt's incarceration, and let him go away. What was to be the end of this he did not know, he hardly cared to guess. There was no light upon the murky landscape. Violet was in prison, and Ursula Dagnell was to reign as sole mistress of Broadlands.

When he was in the train and making for London in hot haste, and, as he thought a little ruefully, on an expedition as wild as anything he had hitherto undertaken, Ursula Dagnell's coming greatness troubled him for a while. Not for himself—for, with all his faults, Tom Dagnell had not been a selfish man—but for poor old Marcus, without an idea in the world that would enable him to get his own living; and for his weak, vain, childish mother, who had not known in her life what a real trouble was, though she had murmured eternally at imaginary cares. There would not be a penny bequeathed away from Ursula Dagnell; in this new-born knighthood of John Dagnell—of the City, very cityish indeed—there were no laws of entail, of primogeniture, to stand in the way of the testator; he had done what he liked with his own, and he had willed all his personal and leasehold estate—and even Broadlands was a leasehold—to his dearly beloved niece, Ursula

Dagnell. Well, it was atonement for his sins of the past, for rash cupidity and speculation, and a greedy hand upon a dead brother's goods —let it stand, thought Tom, as the second good action of his father's life. He, at least, would not utter one complaint against it. What would follow the coming in of his cousin to the Dagnell property, he did not care to think; that lay beyond the present,—when the clouds were drifting, perhaps, and the light was finding its way through to them, proving once again that the uses of adversity were ever sweet and wholesome.

He must settle first—the one mission that was before him, and as he neared London it grew upon him, and absorbed his meditations. All that had happened in the park that morning, faded away like fragments of a dream—his quarrel, if it could be called a quarrel, with Ursula, melted like a breath, and the woman he loved so passionately stepped once more into the foreground of the one romance in life which he had had, or the one reality akin to romance by which his heart had been stirred.

When he was in the Strand, an atom of its roar and bustle and confusion, he knew no more of the nature of the step which he had undertaken than he had done before starting on his errand; he had only felt an irresistible impulse to be acting in some fashion for Violet, and he hoped that, in confronting Hilderbrandt, some good for the daughter might ensue. He had learned of late days a great deal of the character of this man—Violet had often spoken of him at Broadlands—and something from the father's knowledge of the law, even from his cunning in evading it, might be of service in an unlooked-for way.

Tom Dagnell was not long in discovering No. 1109—a medley of a shop that might represent a jeweller's store, a dealer in bric-à-brac, an art collector's, a magazine where choice pictures and statuary, and bad pictures and plaster casts, were heaped together in considerable profusion and without much method. The name of Harnett was emblazoned over the shop front in great gold letters, and registered in black along the brass-work at the bottom of the window, and chastely engraven on the window glass of the door itself, along with various roses, lilies, and birds, emblematic of the rural innocence of Mr. Harnett, possibly, or of his Arcadian tastes. It was a most respectable business, if a little confused; and Tom Dagnell thought he was mistaken, or had been made a dupe by Larry Simes, a youth who might be ungrateful to the last. Still he would prosecute the adventure to the end; and he walked into the shop and was received politely by two or three young men anxious for business, and who suspected a connoisseur in him, and was scowled at by an ugly little Jew traveller, who was displaying samples of jewellery over the counter, with much gesticulation, and endeavouring, vainly, to force a purchase of his goods.

"I tell you we don't want any, sir," said the assistant. "The governor is going to give up business directly. We shall have 'SELLING OFF' in large capitals to-morrow. We are allowing a very large discount to a good customer," he added, with an eye to Tom's future purchases.

"I wish to see Mr. Harnett," said Tom.

"Mr. Harnett. I'm not certain he is to be seen, sir, he has been very ill indeed," replied the assistant.

This bore out Larry Simes's communication to our hero. It was possible that Mr. Harnett was Mr. Hilderbrandt, after all.

"Will you tell him that my business is of great importance, and that I have seen Mr. Larry Simes to-day?"

"Yes, sir. And what name shall I say for yourself?"

"It's of no consequence. Say a friend of Mr. Simes'." The young man departed, and was a long time absent on his mission. The assistants resumed their tasks of invoicing, inspecting and dusting goods; the Jew traveller, with a smothered curse on the slackness of trade, crept with his hand-bags off the premises; an old gentleman, with a grey beard, came in and asked the price of a pair of vases in the window, and went out again; a postman left a whole bundle of letters, which Tom's quick glance detected had foreign stamps affixed to many of them; finally the young man who had acted as his messenger returned.

" Will you please to step this way ?" he said. He led the way through the shop to a side door which opened upon a staircase heavily carpeted, up which he ascended, followed by our hero. At the landing on the first floor, where there were two statues of nymphs holding rose-colour-ed lamps, he knocked, and a woman's voice from within bade them enter.

Tom passed into the room, and the assistant closed the door upon him. It was a first-floor room, overlooking the busy Strand, and close to the window, as though interested in the crowd beneath, and the traffic of the roadway, sat the gentleman with the beard, whom Tom had last seen in the shop making a few inquiries as to the value of two vases. A middle-aged woman, very pale and dark, was sitting at a desk, writing busily, and did not look up as he entered. The room was luxuriously furnished, with a view to customers possibly, as costly works of art met the eye at every turn. On the mantel-piece was china that Mr. Oliver

would have loved to inspect and make a bid
for, and on the walls was a painting—a real
Turner!—which it would have also delighted
Mr. Oliver to see. Tom recognized the painting at once. Yes, this was the den of the
criminal, one of the homes of Paul Hilderbrandt
the prosperous. And this was Paul Hilderbrandt, who took off his beard as he might have
taken off his hat, and waved it politely towards
our hero.

"You are welcome, Mr. Dagnell," he said,
in somewhat of a feeble voice. "You will allow
me to introduce you to my estimable partner.
Mrs. Hilderbrandt, this is our friend Thomas
Dagnell, of whom you have heard me speak
very often."

Mrs. Hilderbrandt's melancholy face was
raised from the desk over which it had been
bent.

"You are welcome, sir. I hope you bring us
good news," she remarked.

"I have come for good news—I thought it
might be possible for you to give me hope of
her," he said, turning quickly to Mr. Hilderbrandt.

The gentleman addressed pitched his false beard into a corner of the room, and regarded our hero with great composure.

"I cannot give you any hope, sir, if you are speaking of my daughter."

"Have you not heard from her to-day?"

"No."

"There are foreign letters downstairs—the postman brought them in whilst I was waiting," said Tom.

"You are observant, Mr. Dagnell. Marie" —to his wife, and with a grave politeness that was somewhat striking,—"do me the favour to touch the bell. Those fellows downstairs will keep the letters till the crack of doom."

He turned to Tom.

"Be seated, sir, I will attend to you in a minute. I——"

He coughed for some time with considerable violence, and Mrs. Hilderbrandt left her desk and stood before him with a glass of some liquid in her hand, watching him anxiously. When he had taken the glass from her hand and drunk of its contents, she walked back to her desk, and recommenced her correspondence.

Mr. Hilderbrandt turned to his visitor.

"I have been very ill—what you English call 'at Death's door,' which is a neat and epigrammatic phrase and signifies a great deal. I am still, sir," he said, somewhat dramatically, "waiting for the door to open, and wondering who will look at me first from the other side. Do you comprehend?"

"Yes."

"They have pronounced my sentence," he said, coolly. "English and French doctors are unanimous in their verdict, and are kind enough to give me six more months of life, if I am careful. You will be sorry to hear this, Mr. Dagnell, for you are interested in my family—but you will be glad to learn that I am careful of myself, extremely careful—always."

Tom Dagnell did not reply—hardly knew in what way to reply to so strange an explanation.

"You will not be disposed to believe me," said Mr. Hilderbrandt, "for antecedents are somewhat against me, but Marie here—Mrs.

Hilderbrandt, I mean—will confirm every word I have said, and Marie always speaks the truth."

" Yes, it is true," murmured the voice in the background ; "but why torture me afresh ?"

" *Pardon, ma chère,*" said Mr. Hilderbrandt, " but I thought I would let Mr. Dagnell know my delicate state of health, lest he should have come to frighten me."

"I have not come as your enemy," said Tom.

"Frankly, I have every confidence in you, Mr. Dagnell," said Hilderbrandt, " or it is not likely I should be sitting in this room with you as my companion. I am very fearful of arrest just now," he added, shrugging his shoulders. "There are terrible draughts in the French prisons. They haven't all the little English comforts of your big model establishments, and the infirmary department is not so well managed as your own, I am told by friends who have tried both. Hence I am particular, and if there had been any real danger I should have shot you sitting there. Ah ! here are the letters."

One of the assistants entered with the letters and tendered them to Mr. Hilderbrandt, who took them from the salver.

"Another time, Jennings," he said, severely, "bring them up immediately, or you will hear from me again."

Jennings departed, and Mr. Hilderbrandt, with an airy wave of his hand, said,

"You will excuse me, Mr. Dagnell, but this is from my daughter, who has business abroad."

"From Violet—at last!" said Mrs. Hilderbrandt, rising from her seat with great precipitation and passing with eagerness to her husband's side again. "Tell me what she says. Let me read it—it is addressed to me, you know."

"Yes," said Mr. Hilderbrandt, handing the letter to her reluctantly, "she does not write to her father—she only preaches homilies to him. Take it, Marie. I would have preferred to read it first.—You are too excitable, and look at life too dismally. Life was not intended to be taken as a black draught; I am convinced of that now. If I could have my time over again

I would enjoy life tremendously. I would drink
life to the dregs."

He passed the letter to his wife, who, in a
manner more foreign than English, pressed it to
her lips and kissed it passionately ere she returned to her desk.

Mr. Hilderbrandt's wandering black eyes followed her every movement; he was regarding
her attentively whilst speaking to our hero.

"I daresay you wonder, Mr. Dagnell, why
my daughter should have deserted a fond, but
a trifle too spasmodic, mother, who had made an
idol of an only child," said Mr. Hilderbrandt.
"It has been always a riddle to me, I assure
you. Why she left me is not so mysterious,
and yet I made an idol of her, too. It was my
own folly; it has brought on us all this
trouble."

"No, no, Paul; it was right for her to leave
us," said the mother, looking up from the letter;
"don't accuse her."

"She has only herself to thank for all that
has happened," replied Mr. Hilderbrandt; "but
why, with nothing on her conscience, she should

go back to France and surrender herself is to me a remarkable proceeding. Who sends the letter?"

" Her advocate," replied the wife.

" Through our friend?"

" Yes."

" You see we have to be cautious, Mr. Dagnell ; we are very artful ; we—Marie!" he cried, suddenly rising and hastening across the room to her, "look up, don't give way! What is in that letter to alarm you? What more bad news is in store for us?"

" Read for yourself," murmured Mrs. Hilderbrandt, passing the letter to him.

CHAPTER VII.

A NEW RESOLUTION.

WHEN Mr. Hilderbrandt had taken the letter from his wife, and was perusing eagerly its contents, his black eyes darting from one corner of their sockets to another with extraordinary celerity, Mrs. Hilderbrandt planted her elbows on the desk and hid her thin face with her hands.

"I wish I could die sitting here," she said, fretfully; "oh! my own girl—my dear, clever, innocent Violet, dragged down to this at last."

"What does that letter say?" demanded Tom, in so imperious a tone that Mr. Hilderbrandt left off its perusal, and the wife, scared from her grief, sat back in her chair to look at him; "read it aloud! Do you think my interest in her is not greater than yours, and more to be considered?"

Mr. Hilderbrandt regarded Tom with evident interest.

"Greater than mine, Mr. Dagnell! Are you quite sure of that?" he said.

"Yes."

"Would you change places with her, if it were possible?" inquired Mr. Hilderbrandt. "Give up your liberty and set her free?"

"Yes, gladly, God knows," cried Tom.

"I wish it were possible," said Mr. Hilderbrandt, malignantly, "for with my daughter here, and you comfortably locked away from her, life would be bearable."

"She had better die than come home," answered Tom; "but what does the letter say? Am I to take you by the throat and shake the information out of you?"

"One moment, sir," said Mr. Hilderbrandt, putting both hands behind his back, "you are too impetuous, and excite my wife, who is of a nervous temperament. 'She had better die than come home,' Marie, do you hear that, and from the man who has brought this accursed trouble on us? For," he added mournfully, "it *is* all through him."

"And Violet loves him—remember that, Paul," said Mrs. Hilderbrandt.

"She says so!—does she say so in that letter?" exclaimed Tom. "Why do you keep staring at me? Why will you not tell me something?"

"It may be a blow to you, if you love my child," said Hilderbrandt.

"If!"

Mr. Hilderbrandt walked slowly back to his chair.

"I will explain at once; and please you to moderate your voice, as my clerks downstairs are not in my confidence, and know nothing of my life. My daughter," said Mr. Hilderbrandt, " declines all assistance from counsel, and will make no attempt to prove her innocence in any way."

" Great Heaven !"

" She will not say a word in her defence."

"She was going to Paris to assert her innocence," said Tom, "to defy her accusers—to——"

"Yes, that is all true," said Mr. Hilderbrandt, checking Tom's outburst, "and she might have been saved possibly. The most eminent advocates in Paris would have fought her battle, not with the money of these Olivers whom you have sent to pester her, and complicate matters, but with *my* money, *my* influence, *my* power. My false witnesses, had it been necessary to lie to save her, should have been there in a legion—she should not have gone to prison. Why, of my black life the girl has never dreamed!"

"She will be found guilty now," moaned forth the mother from the background. "The——"

"Marie, be quiet!" shouted her husband. "You disturb me by your whining—you have become almost a curse to me with your regrets."

"I can't help it," answered Mrs. Hilderbrandt. "Whichever way I look, or strive to turn, is utter misery. What is to be done to save the poor child who——"

"The first thing to be done is to keep your mouth shut," was the very rude remark of Mr. Hilderbrandt; "and the next to listen to me. My daughter," turning to Tom, and beating her letter in the palm of his hand, "has heard, through her indiscreet mother, that I am not likely to live six months, and that half a dozen doctors have been paid large fees to come and tell me so. Hence, as Violet's defence—and those blundering Olivers' instructions,"—he added, as some painful reminiscence of their mediation suddenly occurred to him—"would cast the guilt on me, bring about my arrest, expose me in gaol to hardships and privations to which I am totally unaccustomed, and shorten my days still more prematurely, Miss Hilderbrandt, very kindly and filially, has resolved not to say one word, or give a clue that may interfere with her father's personal convenience. That, sir, is the kind of thing we have at the Porte St. Martin—melodrama of the first class, but infernal nonsense, for all that."

"My poor girl," began his wife. "She——"

"Violet is indiscreet not to save herself at my expense, but I am none the less infinitely obliged to her," the father continued; "and, I may add, proud of her, too, sir. She could not have done more for you, and I am not the lover—the hero—the young gentleman who has known her three months, and made a fool of himself the greater part of the time. I am only the man who has tried to be good and honest in her sight, and failed."

It was bitter satire, but it did not sting Thomas Dagnell in any way, or in any way affect him. He remembered that this man had been an actor, and for some reason or other, difficult to guess at, he seemed acting now the part of cynic.

Mrs. Hilderbrandt was anxious to speak again,—she had even commenced by calling out her husband's Christian name,—when he said, savagely,

"Do you want to kill me by excitement, madam?"

"Heaven forbid, Paul, but——"

"We know the worst, and are resigned to it. Violet saves me, and I die like a gentleman in my bed—like Sir John Dagnell, of Broadlands, who was a scamp after my own heart, though extremely deficient in nerve. You will excuse my allusion to your father," turning to Tom, and bowing politely, "but I am not the only one present who has——"

"I must ask your silence," said Tom, quickly.

"As you please," Hilderbrandt answered, "only don't sit there a grim judge upon me, as if your halo of self-righteousness came to you by inheritance. I know better than that. Your father——"

"Is in his coffin. Let him rest. We are talking of Violet—something must be done," cried Tom; "her life shall not be sacrificed to yours."

"Her own fault," said Hilderbrandt, coolly.

"I will denounce you!" cried Tom.

"What can you say?" said Mr. Hilderbrandt, contemptuously. "I am a respectable and wealthy man. I have never committed a robbery in my life—or raised my hand against my neighbour. I am the proprietor of several vast magazines of art on the Continent and here— all you see around has been honestly bought and paid for—even that admirable specimen of a Turner, Mr. Dagnell, which caught your eye, I perceived, upon your entrance, I purchased for a fair amount of money, although I certainly got it somewhat of a bargain."

"That picture is a witness against you—my word is another," said Tom.

"You will never betray us, and kill him at once!" cried the wife, rising. "Violet will hate you—Violet will——"

"Marie," said Mr. Hilderbrandt, firmly but persuasively, "oblige me by withdrawing. I have a great deal of business to settle with this exuberant gentleman, and you interrupt me sadly. You make me cough my life away—too soon!"

A violent paroxysm of coughing came on as he concluded, but he would not allow Mrs. Hilderbrandt to attend upon him again; he waved her back with his hands; he even rose, walked across the room, and opened the door for her to depart, struggling all the while for breath, and gesticulating vehemently.

"There, there, have patience, Paul, I will go," said his wife; "but when may I return?"

"In half an hour, when this gentleman has gone."

She looked at our hero very earnestly, and suddenly held out her hands to him.

"Good-bye, Mr. Dagnell. Heaven reward you for all your interest in my girl, helpless as it is."

Tom shook hands with her, and she added,

"If I could have altered my husband's life, I would have done it long ago, but I had not the power, so I sank with him. And he is not wholly bad, if you only knew what was in him—what——"

Mr. Hilderbrandt put his hands on her shoulders, kissed her suddenly, fairly pushed her from the room, and locked the door behind her. Tom heard the key turn, and was on his guard, having grave doubts of the gentleman with whom he was locked in.

"Now, sir," said Mr. Hilderbrandt, "we have been losing valuable time hitherto. Take a seat again, and listen to me."

CHAPTER VIII.

BUSINESS.

TOM DAGNELL and Mr. Hilderbrandt sat down facing each other, and the latter said, very quickly—

"You love my daughter? Say it again."

"Yes, I love her," answered Tom.

"She is the daughter of a receiver of stolen goods—over her life will rest the curse of her paternity—and yet you would make her your wife?" said Hilderbrandt.

"I would."

"You are engaged to your cousin at present?"

"The engagement is at an end," said Tom. "But what is this——"

"One moment, and I will explain," said Mr. Hilderbrandt; "my time is as valuable as your own, and I have less of it to spare. I only wish to say that my daughter is worthy to be your wife, and you will find no better, braver girl in the world than she is. There will come happiness," he concluded, hurriedly; "all will be well. I see clearly to the end—to the very end! Shake hands with me, will you, Tom Dagnell?"

Tom hesitated. The man was still incomprehensible; he did not understand him, but there was a new look upon his face.

"Shake hands with me—*her* father! Come, it is your last chance," he said; "I am going away in five minutes."

"Going away!"

"To Paris—to make a full, true, and particular confession of the whole truth, and nothing but the truth," said Mr. Hilderbrandt, lightly. "What is the use of six months of life to me?"

"You will give yourself up?" cried Tom— "you will prove her innocence?"

"Ay, by God, I will!"

VOL. III.   s

Tom seized his hand, and shook it in his own.

"That God will forgive many sins for this one act of atonement!" said our hero.

Mr. Hilderbrandt coughed, struggled with his breath for a while, and then looked with his old sardonic smile at Tom.

"I don't know anything about that," he said; "but here is Violet's life on the one hand, and my carcass on the other—a good name against a bad one, virtue against vice, and the Porte St. Martin business getting to act the fifth. I almost made up my mind to do this yesterday —it was arranged before the letter came this morning, only I was not quite up to the moral standpoint. But Violet has thought of me to-day—I am not the demon to be always shunned, and so I am ready to go. Come with me."

"With you to Paris?"

"You will make sure of me then, for my courage may fail me at the last, without an honest man to stand by. They may release Violet too. They will certainly allow you to see her. Come."

" Yes, I will come," said Tom; " but your wife——"

" She will know all presently," replied Mr. Hilderbrandt. " I wrote her a letter—with full instructions—yesterday, before I had made up my mind. She will go abroad to her friends in Australia. I cannot be distressed by saying good-bye to her now. You saw me kiss her ? "

" Yes."

" That was the last embrace. Come on, Mr. Dagnell; let us get away."

He seized his hat, struggled into an over-coat, and was ready. They went downstairs together, he leaning on Tom's arm, as though he had grown old and feeble suddenly. In the shop, through which they passed in preference to entering the Strand by a side door, Mr. Hil-berbrandt said to his chief assistant,

" Mr. Jardine has not called to-day?"

" No, sir."

" Tell him I have quite made up my mind, will you?"

s 2

"Yes, sir. 'Quite made up your mind,' I think you said?"

"Write it down."

The clerk did so.

"And, by the way, the Turner picture in the drawing-room, I have sold, Mr. Grey."

"Indeed, sir!"

"Will you see that it is sent off immediately to this gentleman's house—packed, and despatched to Mr. Oliver, Elmslie House, Edgbaston, Birmingham?"

"It shall be done at once, Mr. Hilderbrandt."

"Thank you."

Mr. Hilderbrandt and Tom went into the Strand together, and turned in the direction of the South Eastern Railway's terminus at Charing Cross.

"The Olivers were kind to Violet," muttered Mr. Hilderbrandt. "This way—— We shall catch a train. How handy these English railways are!" he added.

He glanced up at the windows above his shop and said, "I don't see Marie. She is very good not to distress me by looking out."

" There is some one at the window above the room we were in," said Tom.

" The devil there is!" he exclaimed. " Ah, she will not think of my being in the streets with these weak lungs of mine—she will not dream of my plans; she has a faint notion of my ideas of comfort. A prison—and a French prison—is not a cheerful place for a rich man to look forward to, Mr. Dagnell."

" No."

" Keep by me," he enjoined. " Keep a tight hold of me, lest I waver at the last. Give me in charge as Hilderbrandt the receiver, if I try to escape. Now then."

When they were at Charing Cross Station there was some excitement on the platform, a bell ringing violently, and the ticket porter just closing the wicket which led to the Dover platform. Tom and Hilderbrandt ran through in great haste, and the latter was fairly exhausted and prostrate when he was by Tom's side in the first-class compartment into which they had hurried.

He recovered by degrees. " What a lucky

thing we caught this train, Dagnell!" were his first words when he had recovered sufficient breath to speak.

CHAPTER IX.

URSULA'S INSTRUCTIONS.

THE four days' leave of absence from the house of mourning had expired, and Tom Dagnell was not back at Broadlands. It seemed as if in the care of the living he had forgotten all thought and reverence for the dead; not a word had come to the old home to tell those within it where he was. It was the day of the funeral; it had been fixed for three in the afternoon, and there were some distant relations of Sir John and Lady Dagnell, and one or two fussy folk from the city expected to the ceremony. It was to be a great, grand funeral in its way, by express desire of Lady Dagnell; and Tom had allowed his mother to have her wish in this as the one best qualified to speak, or as the one most anxious to speak on the question of the pomp and parade which should follow Sir John Dagnell to his rest.

There was an air of bustle about Broadlands that told of business being brisk that morning, and Robin Fisher, in his new suit of black, was extra important, as befitted the occasion. Lady Dagnell was excited, but busy also; the hysterics, and languor, and struggle with the emotions were for a later hour, when the guests were there to see them and to sympathize. At present there was only time to rigorously exercise, lecture and warn the servants of the house. There were two idle folk in Broadlands, however—two who seemed completely bewildered now that the day had come for the burial of the old knight—and these were Marcus Dagnell and his cousin Ursula.

Marcus wandered into every room of the house with his glass wedged tightly in his right eye, as though he were looking for his brother, and hoped to find him in an odd corner; he walked up and down the stairs, and made inquiries of the servants ; he went occasionally to the hall-door, and looked out with vague interest at the sea, across which he thought Tom might be coming presently, and up at the sky, as if Tom's appearance there in a balloon would be on a par with that gentleman's ordinary course of procedure.

Ursula remained in her room, too ill to be of service in the great establishment, she pleaded —too weak to be troubled in any way, she said; too indifferent to the grief and trouble of the house, Lady Dagnell thought, and certainly far too grim and impassive to be fair company. Doctor Smiles was the one individual solicitous about her, and puzzled by her, and inclined to talk mysterious jargon to Lady Dagnell, who had her own complaints too firmly impressed upon her mind to take great interest in her niece's. Lady Dagnell was, on the whole, disposed to believe Ursula's lethargy had been got up to aggravate her, or to elude a share of the responsibilities at this crisis of a sad bereavement. She did not scruple to hint as much to Ursula, who stared dreamily through

the window of her room, and did not turn her
head towards her in reply. Ursula had not left
the window that day—like Marcus Dagnell, the
thought was upon her that Tom might come
back by the sea, and that *The Witch* from Honfleur would bring him home in time. It was
not in her thoughts now that she should never
see him again, and that it had been good-bye
for ever under the green trees. She was waiting for him, she had so much to tell him still in
extenuation of her past, and in proof of her de-
votion. She was much stronger, she thought,
and could reason with him so completely, and
teach him by degrees to forgive her, and—to
keep his word with her! They were all
thinking of the absent member of the family,
at Broadlands, blaming or excusing poor Tom,
according to their various estimates of his
character.

"He was always like this; he was always
running away from home," whispered the
servants.

"It is like his selfishness," remarked Lady
Dagnell. "The house was a blank, and he fled

from it with a paltry excuse, and left this trouble to his mother."

"He is sure to come back," said Marcus, to whom his mother had uttered this last complaint at midday, "the steamer isn't in yet, you know, and the funeral is not till three."

"He will keep away for weeks if he's in Paris. Paris is a very gay place," said Lady Dagnell, sarcastically.

"Ye-es, I wish I was over there," said Marcus, absently.

"Marcus!"

"I mean if I wasn't going to this funeral, of course," said Marcus; "and, upon my honour, mother, I think he'll come, unless he has met with an accident."

"What next will you think of?" said the mother.

"I haven't the slightest idea, but he would have written if—— I'll go and talk to Ursula about it."

Marcus went up to Ursula's room, and asked Mrs. Coombes if his cousin would permit him to pay her a visit, and the answer came in the affirmative, after due inquiry. Ursula was still at the window as he entered, and with the white blind drawn half aside. She beckoned to him.

"I am glad you have come, Marcus," she said, with some little excitement evident in her, at last. "See over there—it is in the distance, I am sure—the steamer from Honfleur!"

Marcus went to her side and looked out.

"By Jove! yes,"· he said, "so it is. I hope he is on board."

" I have prayed all the morning that he might be," said Ursula, "and as I have never prayed in my life before."

" You don't say so—the deuce, now!"

"I was about to send· for you, when you came upstairs," said Ursula, "for you must go down to the quay, and bring him back in the carriage, and tell him I wish to see him very much indeed, and I hope, and implore—implore, Marcus, don't forget!—that he will come and see me, first of all."

" Ye-es, very good; but if we send the

carriage, that will be quite enough, because——"

"Because you are too apathetic," she said,
irritably; "but you must go yourself. I can
trust no one else with such a message."

"Ye-es, very well. What was it I was to
say?"

Ursula frowned at him and repeated her commands, and this time Marcus Dagnell listened
with more attention.

"Do you want me to go directly?" he inquired. "It will take a quarter of an hour to
drive to the quay, and the steamer will be
here in about an hour and a half I should
say."

"You need not leave me," she said. "Sit
down in that chair where the light falls on you,
and let me tell you something."

"Tell me something," echoed Marcus. "I
don't think I care to hear anything more."

"It will come better from me than your
brother," continued Ursula, "and you will be
able to say that I have hidden nothing from
you."

" Ye-es, exactly," said the embarrassed Marcus.

He glanced nervously at his cousin ; he did not admire the steady glance of the grey eyes through the glasses ; he noticed for the first time that Ursula was very ill and wan, and that with her face more strongly lined, and full of deeper, darker shadowings, she appeared to have become prematurely old.

" You don't care to know anything, Marcus," she said, quoting his last protest. " Ah ! because you are not fond of news, and a quiet life is better for your brain. But have you not thought of your fufure position in the world, of how much your father has left you, and Tom, and me ? You are no more unselfish than the rest of the family—you never were unselfish."

Marcus's glass fell from his eye at this ; he was not prepared for so particular a subject.

" I shall know to-day," he replied. " I suppose the will will be read to the family by the solicitor, and so on."

Ursula shook her head.

"Is there anything out of the common in it, then?" he asked.

"Your father had a nervous antipathy to making his will," said Ursula; "he was of the foolish order of mortals, even in that—but at last he did it. Here it is."

And to the further amazement of Marcus Dagnell she produced from a pocket of her dress a long, blue envelope, which she tendered to him.

"You will find the will inside, duly signed and witnessed," she said. "It leaves all to me."

"Eh—what?" and Marcus, displaying more energy and interest than was customary with him, drew the paper from the envelope, opened it and read it through.

"By gad!" was his exclamation when he had completed his task. "So it does."

"There is no other copy of this," she said. "It was written in a hurry, before Tom came back from Honfleur. A solicitor from Arundel was called in to write it at Sir John's dictation. Robin Fisher and Mrs. Coombes were the witnesses to the signature."

"So I see. How the governor must have liked the lot of us," Marcus replied, "to knock off such a will as this!"

"No, he hated me most," was Ursula's reply. "This is no instance of affection, but of Coward Conscience."

"Of what?"

"Ask Tom to tell you the story, when he cares to do so," answered Ursula. "I am not in the mood for it to-day. Have you no temptation to destroy the will—there is no further proof of your father's wishes save this. It is in your hands."

"No," said Marcus, holding it towards her, "here is your document."

Ursula almost snatched it from him, and thrust it into her pocket again.

"You will know some day why this is a just will, and not revenge upon a fretful wife and thankless sons. Where is the steamer now?"

"It's coming on pretty fast."

"Go then—for my sake, Marcus, if you please."

It was earnest pleading, and Ursula seemed strangely moved. Marcus rose.

" I suppose you know that Tom and I have had a few words?" she said, with a forced smile, "not many—but a few!"

"No, I am quite in the dark," replied her cousin.

" Then keep so, Marcus, for the light is very blinding. As for those few words, he will forget them quickly, for he is good, and generous, and forgiving, is he not?"

" Ye—es, I should say so. But I don't know him very well!"

"Is he a good brother, or a bad?" asked Ursula, sharply.

" Oh !——a good fellow."

" If you had done him a great injury, and were sorry for it, very sorry," Ursula continued, " would you expect him to say I will not pardon this?"

" No, I should not. That wouldn't be like Tom."

" Therefore I think, Marcus—indeed I feel sure—that he will cross the sea in yonder ship, and come with open arms to take me to his heart again, knowing there is no happiness for

me apart from him. I am sure he will do this,"
she exclaimed, enthusiastically, "for he is at
heart so noble and so true a gentleman. And I
have not been wholly to blame, Marcus," she
added, "though I have forgiven him everything.
And you will tell him I am very sorry, and ask
him to come to me first of all, to hear me say so.
I shall be watching, and you will give me a sign
that he is with you in the carriage!"

"What is that for?"

"If you can keep the red silk carriage blinds
down, I shall see them, and be prepared for
him," she said, "he will surely come."

"Yes——but what——"

"And that will mean he is coming with complete forgiveness in his heart, now that the past
is irremediable, and that woman is no longer
between us! Then, Marcus, the will will be
heard of no more," she said, eagerly, "it shall
disappear. I want your brother's love, which
was promised me. I never cared for your
father's money—never!"

"But——"

"Go now, the ship is nearing the harbour."

Marcus would have asked another question, but she motioned him to leave her, like a woman too weak and faint to answer another word.

CHAPTER X.

RED SILK BLINDS.

MARCUS DAGNELL was on the quay before the Honfleur steamer had passed through the river's mouth, and ere the sprinkling of Littlehampton visitors, clustered round the lighthouse, had waved their usual salutations to the passengers. Marcus was far from an excitable man, we are aware, but his blood flowed not coldly in his veins that day, and for the first time in his life he could feel his heart beating quick and fast, as if his brother's presence would presage so much to all of them, and his brother's absence forebode the ruin of the family.

He drew a deep breath of relief when he saw

Tom Dagnell standing at the ship's side, waving his hand towards him; he flourished his walking-cane wildly in return, and cut his neighbour across the nose—inoffensive, white-haired, old Mr. Fisher, who had been smiling with placid interest at everything and everybody until that unlucky moment. He had begged to accompany Marcus to the quay, on the box seat of the carriage, and this was the result.

"I beg pardon—really," said Marcus. "But I didn't see you for the moment, Fisher."

"Don't mention it, Master Marcus," he said. "So long as you haven't cut my eyes out, and I can look at him coming home, I shan't mind much. And look there now—Miss Hilderbrandt is with him. Don't you see her? I wish you had not made my eyes water so. Oh! dear."

"And there's Fanny and Slitherwick, and the Olivers," cried Marcus. "By gad, if he hasn't asked the lot of 'em to the funeral."

Yes, they were all there, and looking up at him. Presently they were on the quay

shaking hands with him, and he still bewildered and very much confused.

"Why, I thought—" he began, when Tom
stopped him.

"Yes, yes, but this is no time for explanation."

"But Miss Hilderbrandt——

"Is free, Marcus," cried Tom. "She was
liberated directly her father made a full confession of his guilt. The case against her was
heard yesterday, and dismissed. These French
are quicker than we are, and understand human
nature better," added Tom. "And now, where
is Ursula?"

"Oh! that reminds me," and Marcus deliver-
ed his message, and Tom became graver as he
heard it.

Violet Hilderbrandt, with a face very full of
care still—for with her liberty had not naturally
followed that peace and restful happiness which
were to be hers in the good times—leaned
upon Tom's arm and listened anxiously.

When Marcus had concluded, she said,

"Complete forgiveness she expects from you, Tom."

"I can forgive her bargain with my father," answered Tom; "her deceit to myself—but to turn against you, and——"

"I am going to forgive that. Take me to her."

"It is an unlucky house, this Broadlands," he said.

"I am not afraid," she replied; "and if I may return for a few minutes, and at this sad time, Tom, I should be glad—very glad—to speak to Ursula."

"If you wish it," he said, "it may be for the best, now Ursula is penitent."

They were driven away rapidly to Broadlands, after informing the Olivers and Slitherwicks that Violet should return to them at the hotel as soon as she had seen Miss Dagnell.

It was like coming home again, and beginning life afresh that fair summer's morning, thought Tom—here, at last, was the beginning

of better days for him and Violet—and Ursula!
It was beginning grimly enough, and with the
funeral of his father—but beyond the present
shadows, there might be fairyland in store.

When they were close on the big house,
Marcus Dagnell deliberately drew down the red
silk blinds of the carriage.

" What is that for ?" asked his brother.

"For Ursula," replied Marcus. "She is
short-sighted, but she will see the colour of the
blinds."

" Red is a danger signal, Marcus."

" Yes, I know—but this is arranged between
Ursula and me," Marcus hastened to explain.
" This is security, not danger."

"I understand, I think—but——"

" Don't interrupt me, or I shall forget something," said Marcus. " The red blinds mean to
Ursula that you are coming with complete forgiveness in your heart towards her. That's it,
Tom."

" They were her words ?" his brother asked.

" Yes."

" Complete forgiveness," replied Violet. " No

more reproaches, and some sorrow for your share of all these great mistakes."

"It is just," said Tom, moodily. "But——"

"You must let me see her first, and prepare her for your coming, and pardon her for all the harm she would have brought to me," Violet urged.

"We will go together."

"No—I cannot tell her everything before you," said Violet, looking down and blushing. "I have something to confess myself."

"Very well," said Tom. "Your will is law to me."

"No, no, not yet," cried Violet, turning pale. "And not to be thought of yet, Tom. There is Ursula——"

"No," said Tom, very decisively. "There is no Ursula to forbid the love between us. Because——"

Violet interrupted him in her turn.

"There is my father and his trial, my mother and her future, and to-day is sacred, surely?"

"I am looking forward to the future," answered Tom.

Marcus had sat listening very patiently, but with a confused expression. He was hardly as sanguine as these lovers. Ursula, thin and angular, and with an old woman's look upon her face, rose before him like a ghost which he had lately seen and been scared by.

" I say," he said, suddenly, " don't you think, Tom, if you went to see her first and tell her everything it would be the better plan ?"

" Leave the better plan to us, Marcus," replied his brother. " Ursula is bowed down by grief, tortured by her conscience, horribly grieved that she has doomed an innocent woman to a felon's fate, and Violet will raise her from re-morse by a single word of pardon."

"Yes, exactly; I didn't see it in that light before," answered Marcus, doubtfully. "And here we are, thank goodness."

The carriage passed swiftly round the drive, and the white blind of the upstairs room, which had been drawn aside again, was observed to shake, then drop.

Ursula had seen the signal; he was coming—

it would be complete forgiveness for ever after
this day. Strange, awfully strange, that from
this ghastly funeral time should date so much
of happiness for her. She rose. and swiftly, as
in the old days before she had been struck
down, she passed from the room, and met Mrs.
Coombes in the corridor.

"Tell him in five minutes' time —five minutes
only, and I shall be prepared," she cried.

"Yes, Miss Dagnell—tell whom did you
say?"

"My cousin Tom—he has come back, thank
God! you will find him in the hall. Go—
quick!"

Mrs. Coombes hastened along the corridor
and down the great stairs, and Ursula entered
the room again—or feigned to enter it, for she
stood only within the shadow of the doorway
until her nurse had gone. Then she re-emerged,
and at the same swift pace ran along the corridor into the dead man's room. There was no
hesitation—no nervous fear—as she advanced
to the polished oaken coffin wherein was all that

remained of the old enemy of her peace—the old friend—the old mystery, never more mysterious than in his awful silence and repose.

The coffin was still unscrewed, for it was thought—which was a vain delusion—that many of the funeral guests would like to take a final look at Sir John Dagnell presently. Ursula raised the lid and looked in.

"Forgiveness to you, uncle—and for you, too, I pray. Good-bye."

Under the rigid form she thrust the will which had been made in her favour, smoothed the cerements, replaced the lid, and hurried back to her room, and to her seat by the window through which she had watched her cousin's coming. The old pain in her side returned with double force, but she bore it very bravely. She was happy—her mind was at rest. This was a real self-sacrifice, for which Tom Dagnell would be grateful some day. This would prove to him assuredly that she loved him very much, and was not wholly bad. This Coward Conscience would not let her keep the will. This——

Her train of thought was broken by a light hand tapping on the panels without.

"Come in," said Ursula, rising as she spoke.

The door opened—he was coming—she would go, weak as she was, with outstretched arms to welcome him, and weep upon his breast—it was all happening as she had pictured it!

"Tom, you have forgiven me," she cried, "you have——"

She was silent, struck dumb with surprise and horror, for this was Violet Hilderbrandt before her,—*that woman*, who should have been locked safely from her in a French prison—not free and smiling like this, and at this time!

"You! YOU!" she cried, "how dare you come to me again!"

"All is well, Ursula—I am released—I——"

"Let me pass, woman! Let me pass you, I say—I will not listen to a word," she screamed forth. "I hate you—always! I have been deceived. I must go back and get that paper—I——"

She fell forwards into Violet's arms, still outstretched towards her, struggled away from her, and then sank face foremost on the carpet, and never looked up again, or uttered further word.

*   *   *   *   *   *   *

The funeral was not postponed on account of the serious relapse of Ursula Dagnell. There were doctors attending her, and Mrs. Coombes once more on active duty, when they screwed Sir John Dagnell in his coffin, and carried him and his will away to the cemetery, with a long train of carriages and mourners, to do him a last poor reverence. The next day the blinds were drawn again before the windows, and Ursula Dagnell was not of this world. She had died of severe internal injuries, received on the night she stole down to the sea, it was proclaimed by the doctors, who knew nothing of a heart broken by the sudden shock of despair.

It was not soon that peace came to the Dagnells, left wondering at her fate—or to Violet, and those who in this story may deserve peace, and those fitting rewards which it is in our weak power to bestow. But there was happiness in good time—and it is not in the sunset and with the night coming on that we whisper our farewells.

THE END.

LONDON: PRINTED BY DUNCAN MACDONALD, BLENHEIM HOUSE.

www.ingramcontent.com/pod-product-compliance
Lightning Source LLC
Chambersburg PA
CBHW020856020726
47497CB00005B/1440